Bitter-Sweet, A Reporter's Life

Bitter-Sweet, A Reporter's Life

Arthur M. Merims

BITTER-SWEET, A REPORTER'S LIFE

iUniverse books may be ordered through booksellers or by contacting:

iUniverse
1663 Liberty Drive
Bloomington, IN 47403
www.iuniverse.com
1-800-Authors (1-800-288-4677)

ISBN: 978-1-4917-3505-3 (sc)
ISBN: 978-1-4917-3504-6 (e)

Library of Congress Control Number: 2014910329

Printed in the United States of America.

iUniverse rev. date: 11/07/2014

Preface

This novel was written in ten months between 1960-61 in Paris, France. It reflects some aspects of the author's life as a reporter for the Associated Press in the 1950s. But the work is entirely fictional, especially the romantic portions.

Some aspects of this work were ahead of its time. The "hero" was heavily into exercise long before it became popular everywhere in America. The "heroine" was a career woman at a time when most females were either housewives, secretaries, nurses or teachers.

Reflecting the period, the word "gay" appears in its original meaning. Costs and salaries are low, long before the dollar was strongly inflated. Air conditioning was not as common as it is today. Nearly everybody smoked. Reporters used typewriters and wire services had noisy teletype machines to send the news across the country. There were many newspapers in New York City, the scene of the action.

The novel was originally rejected by three publishers. It was then put aside. It was time for the author to get a paying job, which he did in the field of public relations.

The author was not terribly unhappy about his failure to find a publisher. Life was still new and exciting. He would soon be married, and enter a new career. He had done what he had dreamed of and decided that perhaps he was not destined to be the next Hemingway or Fitzgerald. Still he had gotten to Paris and made the attempt. It was time to start anew.

As the years passed, he felt that this work, while not the Great American Novel, should be available for some to view and perhaps enjoy. So here it is. If you have a few hours to spare, you may be rewarded.

One thing more: my thanks to Tiffany Wilder, who was of great help in getting the pages in shape.

Chapter 1

Jack Stopple had no intention of remaining a bachelor. Like any other normal man, he wanted love and a home of his own and a wife and children: he had said and written that often enough. He dated: in fact he had had several affairs with young women. (These were neglected in his letters home.) But love, that overpowering desire to be with a certain girl and only with her, that had eluded him. Thus far. There was a girl for him, he was convinced, exactly right for him, and his chances of finding her in New York were undoubtedly better than in Oakland, California.

He tightened his grip on the overhanging iron strap as the subway car lurched. Several persons leaned against him in the sway of the train hurtling a curve in the track, steel scraping steel with a prolonged and deafening screech produced by the friction of tons of human and mechanical weight. The air was fetid and warm and his eyes smarted. He wondered if it was nine o'clock yet, but his wristwatch arm was so wedged to his side that he would have had to jab his neighbor to find out. Only a few stations more, he thought.

Perhaps secretly, or even unknown to herself, Mother resented his growing up. She had been opposed to his traveling east from the beginning. But her pique did not give her the privilege of falsely branding him a failure. The charge, particularly in writing, appeared ridiculous. Nine years in New York was inconclusive regarding love or a career. Besides, she was incapable of judging his success as a journalist.

He did not blame her for wanting him to return, especially since his sister had married and gone to live in Dallas. His father had generously offered to set him up with his own book store. But Pops understood that to retire, for that's what it would amount to, peddling warmed-over romances of the Old South to pimply office girls and chauffeured ladies wearing hearing-aids, was inappropriate for a vigorous man of thirty.

As for his job with Intercontinental News, it was a success. Thousands of newsmen would have sacrificed plenty to land a wire service berth in the nation's leading city. And his paycheck was nothing to sneeze at. If he only had a byline. If his folks could see his name over one of his stories in the local newspaper, that might convince them finally that he had made good.

To the public, a byline was journalism's mark of achievement. A reporter without a byline was something less than a reporter, a condition akin to the woman who cannot bear children: though perhaps no fault of her own, it was rather disgraceful. In Jack's department, City News, nobody got bylines; that was the rule, fought out years ago and finally solidified in tradition. His stories ran without a byline, with or without the I.N. slug, or they carried the name of a rewrite man in another department or that of a reporter on one of the local newspapers. But to explain to somebody outside the news trade how arbitrary bylines were was seldom convincing.

His mother's letter was not the only thing troubling Jack as he twisted past people coming off the subway at 42nd street. It was nine a.m. The dull buzz that would be sounding at this instant from the fifty-seven electric wall clocks arrayed throughout the giant newsroom was a sticking pain in his head. Stretching his long strong legs along the pavement crowded with others also hurrying to work, with tourists gawking at the skyscrapers, vendors with balloons, idlers—"excuse me"—"pardon me"—Jack soon reached the entrance to the 38-story I.N. building. The revolving door was spinning already as he whirled through and the elevator whisked him to the ninth floor. He was at least five minutes late.

In recent weeks the pattern had been five or ten minutes, occasionally more. Generally the office was calm at that hour; the pressure to produce news heightened slowly, and he had been unaware of his tardiness. The machine-gun rattle of I.N.'s teletypes never ceased and reporters worked fitfully through the night. With the arrival of the dayshift, the business of news became more of a business. But there had been no warning last Friday when Jackson Johns, the city editor, jerked his hand to motion him forward.

"Why do you come late?" he asked quizzically.

"I…I don't understand, sir."

"You come late to work – have been for weeks. What's up – new girl friend?" He folded his hands behind his head; a half-smile played about his lips.

"No… I hadn't realized it, sir."

"Well… I have a slip here…." Mr. Johns peered at a sheet half-hidden under his desk blotter. "Last Monday you arrived …." He paused to study the figures typed on the copy paper.

"Monday is my regular day off Mr. Johns," said Jack quickly.

"Oh yes? Well, this must be Tuesday. Yes. On Tuesday last you arrived at 9:08 a.m. On Wednesday it was 9:12; Thursday, 9:05 and today I understand you were ten minutes off."

Jack leaned forward to see the slip of paper but Mr. Johns let his blotter fall over it. "Doesn't matter if the figures are exact or not. Point is to get here on the button – nine a.m. is your time, isn't it Jack?"

"Yes sir." Mr. Johns generally arrived at noon; that was "his time," the privilege of being boss. Somebody else then had clocked him and tattled.

3

Mr. Johns cited the union agreement to a "full eight hours," the difficulty of calculating overtime payments, and the danger of giving news competitors "a million dollar advantage."

"But the crux is the public." The city editor jerked his thumb as if at somebody in the distance. "They get cheated. The public has a right to know and the sooner the better. Our job is service, public service. Graft or espionage or sex-slaying or simply a cat up a tree; it's our job to let everybody know about it. Facts, facts. That's our mission. Hit it when it happens." He chuckled half to himself. "If not sooner."

Jack smiled, relieved at the break in the tension. But immediately Mr. Johns' expression changed. "I'm serious. Stopple, deadly serious. Speed is our reputation; we're not going to drop five minutes behind, not for anybody. Get the picture?"

"Yes, sir."

"Good boy."

What annoyed Jack the most was that usually he awakened early enough for a workout in Central Park. There was the root of the problem: somewhere along the line precious seconds of wasted motion had invaded his routine and become entrenched. These had to be weeded out. Ruthlessly. And he was taking pains to do it. By hopping a low wire fence instead of taking the paved path to the reservoir's cinder track he had saved a full minute. Eliminating a second soaping in the shower cut off another fifty seconds. Fewer sprinkles of talcum powder: another twenty seconds. And by strictly minding his own business and refusing to join the other early morning inhabitants of the locker room in their customary but inconsequential gabfest, he believed he had won. On Tuesday and Wednesday, even the subway had cooperated by performing without mishap.

But today he was behind schedule again, and worse, he did not know why. It would be only five minutes or so, but it might be reported to Mr. Johns. Rounding the man-sized filing cabinets that separated City News from Sports, his arms were swinging, his legs churning.

"Owwwwwwwooooooooooo" His sharp yell of pain settled into a low moan as he grabbed his right ankle. The bone had been struck by the pointed toe of a young woman's shoe, the accentuated tip that was the vogue in women's shoes. The shoe's occupant bounced into the filing cabinets, making the metal reverberate dully. She had been exiting from the direction of City News, a batch of publicity releases under her arm, hidden by the height of the cabinets. Clutching his throbbing ankle, Jack's first impulse was to growl, "why don't you watch your step." But seeing her mimeographed sheets scattered on the floor and her open-mouthed mortification, he merely uttered, "Sorry Miss," and picked up her papers. She continued to lean against the cabinets as he handed her the now-dusty releases, appearing to have lost her breath.

She was not pretty, Jack decided at once. A bit too slim, rather boyish and flat. But her sea blue suit with its puff of pink at the throat had style and her narrow piquant face, what he could see of it, was strangely attractive. A white beret that had rested squarely atop her head now covered her left eye and the side of her face so that despite his own discomfort and the awkward situation, her clownish helplessness caused him to grin.

"It's hardly funny," she gasped, her small white teeth in a grimace. She pushed back her hat and fluffed her short coal, black hair revealing a small but jagged scar on her left cheek near her ear, like an ancient knife wound.

"I'm sorry, awfully sorry." With some uneasiness, he was apologizing for observing her scar rather than for smiling or knocking her. But then, despite this momentary diversion, he could not prevent his face from breaking, and, fearing that at any moment he would burst into unaccountable laughter, he hobbled away to his desk and dropped into a chair.

9:08 a.m. He surveyed the office swiftly but could detect no one clocking him. This was deceptive, he knew, since his entrance could have been observed by several without their turning or even glancing his way. It was either Tom Adams, the assistant city editor, or Henry Twist, the chief copy reader. Their workdays

5

began before his, so that each had a daily opportunity to check on his arrival. The other office personnel could be ruled out for a variety of reasons.

As he massaged his ankle, noting with satisfaction that the pain was disappearing, it occurred to Jack that the young woman with whom he had collided might be hurt. He retraced his steps to the corridor, but she was gone. He walked farther along the narrow passageway and looked down the main hallway, but unable to see her, he promptly forgot her.

Jack hung his dark gabardine jacket on the wall rack, straightening its sleeves to preserve its recent pressing, and gazed out the dust-covered window to the street below. Cars and trucks and buses inched along as if to a far off slaughter, now one line spurting ahead of another. Pedestrians scurried over the pavement, between the vehicles, like toys prodded into motion; everybody going somewhere to do something vital, foolish, ordinary, economic, outrageous, propelled perhaps by some mysterious force that originated deep in the city's rock foundation and knifed its way upward through the glistening asphalt. It was a madness this motion that seemed to be a contagion.

Yet when he was out there, among the crowds and the whistles and whirring sounds he could not deny the enjoyment he found allowing himself to be swept along unthinking, unfeeling, unknowing, a part of the whoosh that was a torment and a home.

Suddenly he wanted to be out. The surest path to an outside assignment was to appear eager to work indoors. But he had no patience.

"Morning boss. Got something big for me?" Mr. Adams, chunky and bald, was decidedly not the boss of I.N. City News. He tipped up his green eyeshade and uncovered the harried expression in his bloodshot blue eyes.

"I'm busy Stopple, fly away." He sifted a mountain of publicity releases for news, flinging batch after batch into a stovepipe trash can.

"Isn't there a politician in this city who wants his name in the papers?" insisted Jack. "How about a conference of the Bird

Watchers of America, or the National Congress for Air Pollution Control? Mr. Adams…" Jack lowered his voice…" I'll even take a ground-breaking for a new supermarket."

"Stopple, for a muscle-bound lug who can't come to work on time, you are suddenly mighty eager." He spat into the trash can.

"Are you clocking me? It's pretty low, Mr. Adams. I didn't expect it of you."

"I didn't say it was me. I'm not saying anything at all. I arrive here at eight, sharp. Now stop pestering me, Jack, I have enough to think about."

"Grrrrrr," growled Jack. "That's the growl of an angry tiger, Mr. Adams."

"Sounds more like a pussy cat," he replied without looking up.

Jack returned to his desk and sat heavily. He had been in the office nearly twenty minutes and there was nothing to do. The first hour was always the slowest. Yet they were clocking him. Mr. Johns had been correct in his explanation; still, it was sly and petty and mean. Like the overcrowding. In his nine years with I.N., City News had been squeezed three times as Sports, Theater and Financial expanded. Each time the efficiency engineers had come, standing stealthily in corners jotting cryptic symbols into lined pads. Then, unannounced one night the furniture would be juggled and by morning the aisles were narrower, the desks closer.

"Next we'll be typing in each other's laps," Jack had grumbled after the last consolidation jammed the double row of flat desks back to back. He did not mind the displacement of City News, and judging from the comments, neither did the other reporters. The union protected his job and policy, after all, was up to management. If I.N. decided that home runs were more newsworthy than burning homes, that was their business. Certainly it was more fun analyzing the significance of a movie star's sixth divorce than doing a similar treatment of the city's capital budget. Perhaps the three-point stock rise did merit more comment than the hotel suicide. There were, after all, so many jumpers from hotel windows.

A hand touched Jack's arm and involuntarily it stiffened.

"Hi Scoop. Do ten laps today?" Ann Rawley, the copy girl, tightened her fingers on his biceps.

"Eleven," he replied. "One for you. Say what're you doing?"

"Don't be stingy Jack. I haven't felt an arm like yours since I left home."

Home for 24-year-old Ann Rawley was Reno, Nevada. She had come to New York a year ago and through her father's influence had landed a job, however ignominious, with I.N. At that, it was an accomplishment; I.N. rarely hired women for anything.

"Okay Ann, but enough is enough." He brushed her hand off and to his chagrin felt the flush deepen in his cheeks.

"How touching! Love blooms in noisy news rooms. The pulsating palm caresses the brawny arm. I feel a poem coming on: crawling with arms, legs, naked limbs of course. Highly moral verse. Spiritual. About today's crop of young lovers. Note the farm angle." Stanley Cowels ducked behind a tabloid but he appeared to be awaiting a response as eagerly as a schoolboy who has just pulled the braids of the girl in front.

"Mind your own business, dirty old man," snapped Ann. Her vehemence surprised Jack.

"Unkind. Cruel. Heartless. Callow. What is becoming of our innocents? Nobody has ever called me old, Miss Rawley. Even my two-headed sons are better trained. I am the spirit of youth, the flower of boyhood, the essence, my dear, the very essence. I am younger than young Stopple here. Ah, if you only knew me, Miss Rawley, if you only cared to know. If you only cared…. Also, I bathe regularly."

She glared at him. "You also pinch me regularly and if you don't stop I'm going to tell Mr. Johns." Like a filly she tossed her long straight blonde hair that habitually strayed over her eyes.

"I am not now, nor have I ever been a molester," he declared haughtily. "Of course, if you insist on crowding my desk when you pass on your missions of malevolence, my only recourse is self-defense." He ducked behind his newspaper again.

Ann turned to Jack. "I'm having a party at my place tomorrow night," she said. "Will you come?"

Cowel interrupted. "Yes, yes, of course I'll come. So nice of you to ask me. I'll bring a bottle of Chianti. I'll wear my flowing red tie."

Ignoring him, she edged closer to Jack and tempered her voice. "There won't be much drinking or smoking this time, I promise. Can you make it?" She lifted her eyebrows, wrinkling her forehead; the lines disconcerted Jack; someday they will be there naturally, he thought. But he replied simply that he already had an appointment.

"I've got an air conditioner, "she exclaimed, brightening. "Forgot to tell you. It's guaranteed to clear the air as well as cool it. Honest. Besides, you haven't been to one of my parties in ages. I need new blood. Are you angry with me?"

"No, of course not." Jack arose and backed away slightly.

"Oh yes," she added. "There's somebody wants to meet you. A girl. I told her how you believed in health and exercise and all that and she said she was very interested too."

"Rare for a girl to be interested in that," he thought aloud.

"Not bad looking either," noted Ann. "Maybe you saw her. She left as you were coming in this morning."

"Her? The skinny girl … with the white beret?"

"Yes. Do you know her?"

He laughed softly. "Well, we met informally."

"Oh? She's not your type anyway."

"Why not? What's her name?"

"Never mind. Come and find out."

"Okay." He laughed. "You got me, if I can bring a friend. I had a date with him."

"Sure. As long as it's a 'him.' Come after nine." She walked off, swinging her hips and arms as if she were sauntering through a field. As Jack picked up a newspaper he observed Cowels' eyes following her to the rear of the department. An amusing discovery. Cowels wanted her, but she apparently found him repulsive. She, it seemed, favored him, but he, Jack mused, had no desire for her. The perversity of human nature: wanting what you can't have, ignoring what is here and now.

Perhaps he was foolish for ignoring her obvious interest in him. Opportunities were to be taken. But finding girl friends had never been Jack's problem, so another easy conquest succeeded only in making him feel cheap. Moreover, there was an intrinsic honesty about Ann that prevented him from being dishonest. She was what they called "a good kid," wholesome, pleasant, fair, fun to be with, yet lacking in a certain feminine charm that attracted men. Her face was a bit too round, like an apple, her mouth too wide, her figure too full. But her blue eyes were alive and gay and altogether she seemed warm and friendly. Even if she was a little plain and rash and noisy, Cowels was showing sense in his pursuit.

A thump on his shoulder made Jack aware of his neighbor leaning toward him. "Jackson," whispered Cowels, "you don't have to answer if you don't want to, but if you do, I'd appreciate the truth: are you making her?"

"Ann?" Jack stalled. "What do you mean?"

Cowels hunched his shoulders; his dark eyebrows crowded his eyes. "Oh come off it boy. I know she's hot for you. Have you got her sowed up or not?"

Jack swung around on his swivel chair to face him, purposely delaying his reply. He liked Cowels, who, while considered the office "character" was also perhaps the best I.N. rewrite man. He was completely gray, but his hair was beautiful: thick and wavy and bunched in the back like an artist's. He never wore a necktie, seldom a suit.

Instead, he favored a black turtle-neck sweater. His dress was a direct challenge to management, which insisted that its reporters be attired in conservative business suits, white shirts and a tie. But Cowels brandished his costumes like weapons. A crisis had passed years ago and Cowels had won, a limited victory to be sure. He could dress as he pleased, but he was forbidden to leave the office on assignment without the "regulation uniform."

"She's not my girl, Stan, if that will help."

"It may, pal, it may. Thanks."

Jack swung around in time to hear Mr. Adams call him. As he rose to learn his first assignment he heard Cowels say dryly, "See you at the party."

Chapter 2

The thick gray marble and brick walls of the criminal courthouse signaled stern justice. But neither its dirt-encrusted exterior studded with iron-barred windows nor its dimly lit corridors intimidated Jack. He had worked there too often.

He eased through the revolving door, nodded to the uniformed guard at the information desk and strolled to the press room. It appeared as if the occupants had fled: rock 'n' roll blared from a small radio, the fluorescent lights burned, the air conditioners hummed; scattered on the flat desks in disarray were several crumpled newspapers, coffee containers, pencils, piles of copy paper and a half-eaten sandwich partially wrapped in wax paper. But in the narrow locker room in back the daily poker game was underway. Jack recognized some of the reporters, attorneys, bail bondsmen, and a few returned his greetings with a swift glance or a turn of the head. One of the players, his wooden chair tilted on edge, was Magistrate Martin P. Goodworthy. It was a rather silent, intense game, with quarters, halves and dollar bills changing hands with the speed of busy cashiers in a midtown automat. Jack watched awhile, but soon became bored and left for his assignment, felony court.

Down the center aisle of the high-ceilinged courtroom, past the public benches crowded with friends and relatives of the defendants, complainants, and other spectators, past the waist-high oak barrier that separated the audience from the court participants, a youth in dirty blue dungarees and a tee shirt stood sullenly, his head cocked to one side, as a clerk read aloud the charge against him: statutory rape. The alleged victim, a stubby frizzled blonde, clutched his hand and leaned her head against his shoulder. Her mother pleaded with the jurist to dismiss the charge.

"You see, your honor, they're gonna get married now," the woman said in a forced whisper, "so everything is all right."

"The wedding settles everything, is that what you mean?" Presiding Magistrate John C. Freeman was frowning.

"Yes, your honor, that's it exactly," she said eagerly.

"You've done your duty by your daughter, is that it?" the Magistrate continued.

"Yes, that's it exactly," she responded. But now her tone was unsure.

"Your daughter is 15 years old and the defendant is 17, and they're going to get married and live happily ever after, is that how you see it?" His irony and anger was unmistakable.

"I certainly hope so, your honor, I certainly do. They love each other, your honor, and I certainly wish the best for them." She spoke swiftly, twisting a tiny handkerchief in her hands.

"Is that why you initiated the charge of rape against the defendant, this serious accusation of rape? Is that how you wish the best for them?"

"Well, your honor, that was before... before he wanted to marry her. He was wrong, your honor; that is, they were hasty." She dabbed at her eyes. "I had to protect my daughter, your honor. Even though she wants him I had to protect her. That was my duty your honor, as a mother. I only did my duty."

"You have done your duty, madam, but I must also do mine. The offices of this court cannot be abused. This is a serious charge and I will not dismiss it." However, after setting a date for a hearing, he paroled the defendant without bail.

"God bless you, your honor," the woman cried. And the three hurried out together.

"Are you legal aid?" the court clerk asked Jack as he entered the area of the proceedings.

"No," he replied. "I'm a reporter."

"Is legal aid here yet?" the clerk shouted to the courtroom. When there was no response he called the next case.

Johnny Hogan, a big burly reporter with a barrel chest, rested his elbow against a partition near the magistrate's raised platform. Hogan, who looked more like a cop than do most policemen, had worked the precincts and courts for twenty years. His description of the electric chair execution of Hans Conway, ax-slayer of three women, had won a national award.

"You ain't missed nothin'" he said. Then he added, "good stuff's comin' up – playground killing."

Magistrate Freeman hurried the arraignments. After a cursory glance at the complaint papers, he invariably asked the arresting officer, "What date?" The cop never responded with a "date" but named the soonest day convenient for him to be back in court. The magistrate usually fixed that day for a hearing on the charge and then set bail for the defendant. It was a dull session: barroom assaults, wife beatings, stolen cars, dope addicts, thieves, homosexuals. Jack doodled with his ballpoint pen. Despite the court rule against reading newspapers during the proceedings, Hogan sneaked glances at the racing section. Then he nudged Jack.

"You comin' to the club ball this year? It's the 23rd of next month. I got tickets."

"Don't know yet. How much?"

"Fifty bucks a couple. Same as last year."

"Jesus. Who do they think we are?"

"Aw, don't you have friends?"

"Not fifty bucks worth," admitted Jack. "You?"

"What you take me for?" Hogan cupped his hand and whispered, "Guess who's takin' me this year?"

Jack shrugged.

Hogan nodded toward the bench.

"Freeman?" inquired Jack.

"His honor himself. But don't let it get around, huh?"

Jack shook his head. "I.N. keeps me moving too much."

"Yeah, well keep tryin'. The club wants as many workin' stiffs as possible this year. The guest list is getting' outta hand. If you buy from me, I guarantee a good table."

They stood and waited. So much of a reporter's life was waiting. Outside shut doors, in corridors, on street corners, in smoke-filled rooms, in luxurious clubrooms, waiting for the official pronouncement that made the news. "He confessed. Yeah, at 2:34 p.m.. He did it; he said so." Bulletin, bulletin. "We are troo negotiatin'. If dats da way day wanna slice it, dats da way it's gonna be. Da strike is on, as of right now." Rushing for the telephone. "City desk please, and quick." Waiting for the word. From the meeting, the conference, the grilling, the court, the legislature, the political headquarters. "He is studying the issues and will make a statement as soon as possible," the spokesman said, the attorney said, the executive said, the assistant said, the reliable source said, the official said. Somebody always had something to say; after the waiting there was the word.

A black-clad woman shrieked from the rear of the courtroom and rushed forward as a boy and a girl were led from the detention room.

"This is it," noted Hogan, suddenly alert like a hound who has sniffed his favorite scent. Jack pulled out a scratch pad as the court clerk read aloud the charge: homicide. The pair were accused of shooting a 16-year-old companion in a west side playground, inflicting stomach wounds from which he died en route to a hospital.

"Are you related to these defendants?" the magistrate asked the woman.

"He's my son Anthony your worship," she replied, hugging the boy about the shoulders. "He's my boy, my only son, oooooohhhhhh." Her moan flooded the room.

"Now stand behind him and be silent madam, or I will be compelled to eject you from the court," the magistrate commanded. "Do you understand?"

The woman nodded, wiping her eyes with the loose ends of a long black kerchief covering her head.

"On this charge," in a swift almost incomprehensible monotone the court clerk began his routine spiel, "you have the right to communicate by letter or telephone to friends or relatives free of charge, the right to an adjournment to get a lawyer, to bring witnesses, to have a hearing in this court. You can waive further examination for the grand jury. What do you want to do?"

Jack scribbled a description of the girl, abbreviating words, leaving out punctuation, connectives, articles, prepositions; her thin rouged face and purple-lipsticked lips; her red-dyed hair, its dark roots showing, cut like a boys, jagged edges; wearing slacks, open shirt; her eyes defiant, bitter; the other defendant, Anthony, in cords and tee shirt, well-built like a weight-lifter, his dark hair swept back, trying to appear tough, unconcerned, slouching.

"You there, hands out of your pockets," the magistrate boomed, his ruddy face coloring deeper as he rose slightly from his seat, his shoulders quivering under his black robe. "Stand up straight. Both of you. You are in a court of law now and don't forget it."

The mother moaned again and shook her head from side to side as if she were arguing with herself.

"Any other relatives or friends of the defendants in court?" the magistrate called out. When there was no response he asked the arresting officer if both families had been notified. The policeman said yes.

"Do you have a lawyer?" asked the magistrate.

The defendants remained mute. "No lawyer, no money," the woman sobbed.

"Please control yourself madam," he said. "I'm going to give you a lawyer, temporarily, without cost." He motioned to one of several attorneys who attended felony court daily to pick up stray cases. The lawyer took the defendants and the mother to a side of the room reserved for consultations and the case was set aside momentarily. When it was recalled, the lawyer announced that he had informed them of their legal rights; then he asked the magistrate to parole the defendants on bail. The assistant district attorney, a young man with blond crew-cut hair and rimless eyeglasses, argued that the nature of the charge prohibited bail. But the court-appointed lawyer countered that neither defendant had a police record.

"Now the girl, your honor, she wasn't even present when the alleged shooting took place," he added.

"What?" exclaimed the magistrate? "Then why is she accused?"

"She's the motive, your honor," volunteered the arresting officer.

"The motive, the motive. How fascinating!" The magistrate pressed his lips together and scratched the back of his head. "Cherchez la femme. How efficient our police force is to uncover motives as well as criminals."

"She was involved, your honor," the policeman said. "They acted in concert."

"And I'm sure they made beautiful music together," noted the magistrate dryly. There was a tittering among the spectators.

"Let's have order here. Quiet down." He turned in his chair to face the policeman. "Will you tell the court, if you can, how she motivated the death of a 16-year-old boy."

"She was the girl friend of the accused, your honor," the policeman said. "Then she switched to the other kid, who is now the deceased...."

"She never switched," shouted Anthony. "He stole her from me."

"Silence you," boomed the magistrate. "You've done your work. Now be still."

"The girl," added the policeman "gave him the gun."

"Is the weapon in court?" asked the magistrate. The gun was handed up to him. "Interesting. An ordinary hunting rifle, the kind anybody can purchase in a sporting goods store. Except the barrel has been sawed off and the stock cut down."

"My Anthony don't have no gun, mister judge, he's a good boy. He go to church with me every Sunday," cried out the mother.

"Again I must ask you to control yourself madam. We are not trying this case. This is merely an arraignment. We cannot permit outbursts in this court." The magistrate spoke gently and somewhat absentmindedly as he examined the legal documents. The court waited in silence. After a few moments he raised his head; his gaze wandered toward the reporters, stopping on Hogan. Jack nudged his companion who looked up at the magistrate. Then the jurist turned to the defendants.

"This is a serious charge, the most serious possible," he began, his voice low but resonant with emotion. "I don't know what's happening to our youth, what makes them value life so cheaply. When I was a boy children were taught not to raise their voices, much less their fists. Girls learned how to sew and cook and clean house. Playgrounds were for skipping rope and baseball. Now they are for gang fights and murder."

He savored the last word as the reporters scribbled in their own shorthand, trying to get every word.

"People blame the war," the magistrate continued. "The war has destroyed morality and the sickness has infiltrated society down to our infants. That is too easy. We have always lived in wartime or between wars. But we have never condoned violence and evil. Perhaps there is a chaos afoot, a corruption that we cannot see or feel but that is infecting and destroying us.

"Are the parents to blame? Too busy perhaps. Too concerned with themselves, too confused to care for their children. The breakdown of family life...." His voice trailed off. He rubbed his eyes with the fingers of one hand. A cough from the public benches broke the silence. Then he spoke again, softly, as if to himself....

"What is the motive for firing lead into a boy's stomach? Love? Is that the motive here? Love between a boy and a girl: was it once a shy thing, a tentative thing? Something a girl blushed about and a boy suffered in silent questioning? But that is so old fashioned, isn't it? Children seem to 'go steady' shortly after they turn in their diapers; they're not content with bashful kisses, no, they want passion, sex, possession of body and soul, even before they know how to spell. In such a hurry to live, and die."

The defendants stood impassive, seeming neither to see or hear the magistrate. They appeared to be staring through him to the flags of New York State and the United States draped in the rear.

"Is there no evil left in your world?" the magistrate shouted suddenly. "No ethics? No morality? Is violence the only thing that makes you alive?" The magistrate had grasped the thick wooden arms of his chair to prevent his quivering. Then he sank back, as if all the energy had flowed out of him.

"I don't know where it began or where it will end," he concluded. "But murder is not juvenile delinquency. One thing I can tell you kids, the courts are not going to slap your wrists and let you go. I'm holding the defendants for a hearing next Tuesday. No bail."

Court attendants led the youths back to the detention room. The woman tried to hold on to her son. "Why you do these things?" she cried. "Why you do these things?" A guard pulled her back and guided her toward the exit. The reporters followed her into the outside corridor, firing questions.

"What gang does your boy belong to? Does he work or go to school? How long has he known this girl?"

"No gang, no gang," she replied. "He's a good boy, he works in a supermarket."

"Does he always carry a gun?" demanded Hogan. "Or a knife, a switchblade?"

"No gun, no knife," she cried. "Who are you?"

"District attorney's office," snapped Hogan.

A photographer held his camera ready. "Can you hold still a minute fellas?" he pleaded.

"No pictures. I don't want pictures. Get away from me," she said angrily through tears. She raised her right arm as if to protect herself. The photographer shuttered his camera. The photo appeared the next morning in the "Daily Globe" under the caption, "Defiant mother of accused youth slayer."

Court police entered the corridor. "Quiet down here," said one. They took the woman aside and the reporters hurried downstairs to the press room. Word of a good story had preceded them; the card game had broken up and several newsmen asked to be filled-in.

"Okay, okay. Shut up everybody," shouted Hogan. "Let's organize this. I'll go through the whole thing slowly." Then he reconstructed the court scene, reading from his notes, while the others copied. He reviewed the magistrate's speech.

"...Violence is the only thing that kids enjoy," Hogan read from his pad.

"I've got it as a question," noted Jack. "Is violence the only thing that makes you alive?"

"No, I had that right," asserted Hogan. "Besides, it's more powerful as a statement than a question. It'll make a good lead."

"I'm sure he asked a question," argued Jack.

"I've got it right here." He pointed to his notes.

"How about, 'now violence is the only thing kids live for'," suggested a reporter who had been in the poker game.

"Okay, we'll compromise," declared Hogan. "Got that everybody, 'now violence is the only thing kids live for'."

Jack hesitated. It was a small point, but he was certain he was right. Still, if he bucked the others, they would consider him a prima donna, a glory seeker. And if he called in the quote without telling them, he would be a sneak. His duplicity would be remembered if he ever needed help. Then he would be snubbed. Well, it was a minor detail. Magistrate Freeman would not object. Jack altered his copy.

When Hogan finished, he answered questions until every aspect had been reviewed. Then he said, "Okay guys. We'll call in…" he looked at the wall clock "… in 14 minutes, at exactly 12:20."

"But I've got a deadline now," a reporter complained.

"Shit, you weren't even there --- what are you squawkin' about?" replied Hogan.

The reporters settled at their desks, quietly reviewing their notes. Each had a private telephone direct to his office. At 12:20 p.m. they began calling.

"I've got a good one," Jack told Mr. Adams. "Boy killed in a playground. Two accused – looks like a love story – eternal triangle – ha, ha, very funny – don't ask me why they do it."

Chapter 3

His day in the criminal courthouse hung heavy on his shoulders and as Jack climbed the narrow stairway to his top-floor apartment he realized he was stooping. Shifting the loaf of bread and container of milk to his right arm, he straightened his back and lifted his head. "Posture makes the man." He repeated the phrase to himself in rhythm to his steps.

Jack lived in a one-and-a-half room flat in one of the many brownstones in Manhattan's west 80's that years ago was converted from a private family dwelling to furnished rooms and small apartments. Through the thin partitioned walls Jack often overheard his neighbors; but he rarely spoke to them. In this, he was not unique; anonymity and privacy were respected in a crowded city: you could never tell whether you had anything in common with your neighbor beside an address.

The iron-engraved nameplates had disappeared, replaced by slips of paper with scrawled handwritings. Now it was a transient community; not that its inhabitants moved continually; housing was too scarce for that. But the West Side was occupied mostly by people between worlds: Puerto Ricans and Cubans recently from the islands, immigrants from Germany, Poland, Hungary, Rumania; Negroes escaping their Harlem ghetto or the South, drifters from the middle west, retired folks without families, and many young single people, like Jack, who had left their home towns for the opportunities in a metropolis.

It was a neighborhood of second-hand cars and stray cats that hissed and howled in the night, of gray drawn women sitting like stones in bare windows, of children of varied colors and races shouting in the streets, of cha-cha-cha blaring in the night and cries of "help" mingling with "lower that goddamn television." No questions were asked and few complaints made because nobody intended to remain. Jack, too, planned to move to Queens or Long Island when he married. Though eight years had passed, he still did not feel a member of the community. His work kept him downtown and his few friends were scattered about the city. He remained because better apartments were still scarce and expensive and because he felt there were advantages that outweighed the run-down condition. Subway and bus lines were handy to speed him to work. (He rarely drove his Plymouth downtown to buck the heavy traffic and compete for the few parking spaces.) Central Park was across the street and nearby, too, was the Hudson River.

The key turned stiffly in the lock and as he swung open the door stale air twitched his nostrils. The stubborn Scottish landlady who brought up the mail and cleaned perfunctorily had shut the windows again. Despite his instructions to the contrary. She insisted that only dirt entered. He flung up both windows and breathed deeply, stretching his arms sideward in cadence until with a vigorous motion he struck the wall. "Damn it," he cried, and blew on his tingling fingers.

Of the three letters on the wooden folding table that served also as a kitchen table, one offered a magazine subscription at reduced rates and another advertised a new rug cleaning service. He tore them into small pieces. The faded green throw rug beside his bed needed more than cleaning. The third letter was from Mahoney and Kahn, his brokerage firm, advising the purchase of a "deflated" oil stock. A handwritten message read, "For your info. Bill." Jack stuffed it into a bureau drawer crammed with printed matter. He was fixing dinner when Sally telephoned; she wanted to come up.

"Please don't," he said firmly.

Speaking rapidly, her voice cracking occasionally, she apologized "for last time." She had been upset, "something I ate," and also had fought with her father. But she wanted to see him tonight.

"There isn't anything more to say." Jack closed his eyes and massaged his forehead. "We'd only hurt each other again. I'm sorry Sally, but it's over."

She continued explaining. "I didn't say it was your fault," Jack interrupted; it was embarrassing to hear her plead, but he knew it would be foolish for him to weaken. If she came up he might make love to her, just because she was available, knowing full well there was nothing lasting between them. "It's probably my fault," he said. "Yes … but that would be a waste of … No …Yes, I'm sure it can't … Goodbye dear.…"

He held the receiver away from his ear, listening to her voice without understanding the words; it was like an old scratch gramophone record. Then he replaced the receiver on the hook. He plopped into the easy chair and sighed wearily.

It was cruel to cut her off, yet it might have been worse to bend to her arguments. The truth was that he had never loved her. He remembered the Labor Day weekend last fall at the Green Hills Country Club, backstroking away from shore, his head cool in the lake water, the green pines like a painting against a cloudless blue sky, when his sweeping arms struck rubbery flesh and suddenly they were entangled, laughing and struggling. Swiftly they swam together, bubbling nonsense and teasing; she had touched him beneath the water and they kissed.

He remembered the crowded dance that evening, after the starchy dinner and the variety show, suddenly she was beside him, daring him to buy her a drink. The moon was shrouded in mist when they stumbled over pebbles on the grassy path to the cabins. She led him directly to her room and locked the door and the odor of heavy perfume fused with pine; the cots were unmade. They were still lying naked, when her roommates banged on the door. She said to come back later and one complained that she was "completely exhausted" and wanted to go to sleep "now." He had offered to climb out the window but she insisted he stay and she refused to let them in. He remembered being startled when they swore.

But in the city, in his small apartment that had neither the smell of pines nor the romance of an exotic atmosphere, they found little to talk about; so they did what required little talk and obscured their separateness. Taking her home afterward was not a carefree tripping along a neat tree-lined path but a long stuffy subway ride to Forest Hills or an equally fatiguing automobile trip. With the sunset hidden behind towering gray buildings and the chirping starlings drowned out by grinding gears and police sirens, their golden hued romance disclosed its brass base.

She became bossy, and at the most inopportune moments. She insisted he profess his love for her when they were in bed, but when he did so, grudgingly, she was unsatisfied. She wanted to know if he "really" loved her, and, aware of his deceit, he could never make yes sound convincing. When, in annoyance he responded "NO," it was worse; then she would want to go to the theater or a movie or a nightclub, insisting, while they still lay unclothed, as if demanding a sort of payment.

She smoked like an addict; he did not object to occasional cigarettes; everyone could not be expected to be as health conscious as he. But she was a compulsive chain smoker. In desperation he swamped her with clippings on the danger of lung cancer, but, if they had any effect, it was to make her smoke more.

Their meetings had less meaning and the number of arguments, usually over inconsequential things, increased and became more stormy. The breakup came two weeks ago. "You deceived me, you lousy bastard; all you wanted was my body," she shouted. He slapped her across the face and she burst into tears. But it was too late to be sorry; she bored him and he was truly happy it was over.

Jack resumed his cooking chores; he flipped on the television set. A syrupy voice announced, "and now, Mark Larson and the Local News." Jack turned from a can of asparagus he was prying open to watch the screen: a lean grim-faced man with dark curly hair and thick black eyebrows appeared to be staring directly at him. But Jack knew the man must be reading a script in large lettering on a prompting machine immediately adjacent to the television camera.

"Good evening ladies and gentlemen. Teen-age crime again took the spotlight in New York today with the arraignment of two youths, one a 15-year-old girl, accused of the brutal slaying of a boy, possibly a rival gang member. The shooting, in a west side playground, had some of the aspects of a love triangle. The victim…"

In rapid-fire ominous tones the television reporter detailed the courthouse scene that Jack had covered earlier. Then there was a commercial for hair tonic, after which Mark Larson described the mayor's press conference.

"… and that's the news I covered today," he concluded.

The screen held his watery smile several seconds, then it was replaced by an animated cartoon advertising a liquid cleanser.

"You got reason to smile." Jack spoke to the television set. "The closest you came to that court story was your teletype machine."

He had finished dinner and was sipping tea with honey and lemon when his friend, Bill Meyers, telephoned.

"Get that tip on Minnesota Oil?" he asked.

"Yes," replied Jack. "Anything to it?"

"The office likes it but I don't. What you doin'?"

"My night for the 'Y'. Want to work out?"

"No. But I've got nothing better to do. Meet you in the lobby."

Bill first met Jack during their fraternity pledge night and almost immediately they became friends. They were the same age and in the same college year on the Berkeley campus; both were in the journalism school and both worked part-time for the "Daily Californian," the student newspaper.

Those were the turbulent post-war years when thousands of war-hardened veterans had returned to school. An older, generally more serious group, many with wives and children living in makeshift housing, they were determined to catch up with civilian life in a hurry. Bill, running for president of the junior class on a political platform that promised more social activities and greater emphasis on athletics, was defeated by an ex-paratrooper who demanded housing, civil rights, and increased benefits for veterans.

Jack, a member of the basketball and track teams, was a popular figure on campus, though he took little interest in activities other than sports and his studies. But in their senior year, Bill persuaded him to be his running-mate as he campaigned vigorously for the office of student body president on a "Throw Out the Radicals" platform. They won by a narrow margin and decided during a beer and pretzel celebration party that they were an unbeatable combination. In this spirit they planned to "Beat New York" after graduation. Though their families did not share their enthusiasm for an eastern invasion, they were persuaded by their youthful spirit of victory. Besides, the news capital was New York, and the boys wanted to experience living in the city they had heard so much about but had never seen.

They arrived at the 34th street Greyhound bus terminal and after a brief stay at the Sloane House 'Y' they found a tiny apartment in Greenwich Village. Jack's second attempt at job hunting was Intercontinental News where a pretty blonde receptionist cheerfully said that I.N. "never hires anybody with less than five years reporting experience." But, perhaps impressed by his six-foot sturdy bearing or his straw-colored hair that flopped over his forehead, she accepted his application. A week later he received a letter for an appointment with Mr. Jackson Johns and after an interview was asked to fill out more documents, in triplicate. His credentials would be verified, he was told. Two weeks later he got the job. Several months afterward he learned that he had applied in the very week I.N. decided to break precedent as a cost cutting experiment and that at least forty college graduates were considered for the lone position.

But Jack's phenomenal success was not matched by his roommate. After eight weeks at newspaper and wire service offices, Bill was exhausted, discouraged and also heavily in debt to his friend. In a desperate effort to earn some money while awaiting his break in journalism he began a paid training course with a brokerage house. To his surprise he discovered that he enjoyed the intricacies of the securities markets. Six weeks later he found himself a fledgling stock broker with a new desk and two telephones and several dozen leads on prospective clients. The more he studied the stock market the more he developed a certain flair for it, and though he disliked the aspect of selling to strangers, he was pleased by his success and decided that he had a heretofore hidden talent for speculation. When finally a local newspaper invited him to apply as a copy boy, he burned the letter before Jack with a great flourish.

After a year, both felt economically secure enough to afford better living quarters and they decided to get their own apartments. There had been no rift in their friendship; on the contrary, as strangers to the city, they had drawn closer. But both had become involved with girls and wanted the privacy to continue their romances at their own convenience. Neither cared to remain in the Village, disliking the odd characters they met there, and so they gave up their apartment.

As Jack arrived at the revolving door entrance to the 'Y' two boys were chasing each other around and around, making the glass panels spin like an egg beater. He waited, but when their game became more reckless, he collared one like a puppy.

"Huh," the boy said startled. Jack released him as his companion slowed the door to a halt.

"We were only having fun," said the boy, recovering his poise. "Sure," muttered Jack, and as he started in, they shouted, "killjoy," and fled.

The dimly-lit lobby was tinged with the faint sweet odor of sweat. A few youths bunched outside a telephone booth but otherwise, the huge hall resembled a church at midnight. Bill shook Jack's hand and pointed to the bulletin board.

"Professor Heinrich is lecturing here Tuesday night on 'the art of doing'."

"Doing what?" asked Jack.

"Doing, that's all. You pay a buck twenty-five to find out what."

They flashed their membership cards to the basket room attendant and removed their gym clothes to the locker room. Bill fumed as he failed to open his lock.

"I'm sure I've got the right numbers," he said.

Jack offered to help. "All the locks have the same formula." Jack turned the dial and on the second try the small steel bolt sprang ajar. "Easy," said Jack.

"Guess I'm just an artist – not a mechanic."

They grinned. Bill was several inches shorter than his friend and his flabby chest and beginnings of a paunch contrasted sharply with Jack's hard muscular frame.

"Don't look so disapproving," said Bill as they stripped. "Can't become Charles Atlas sitting on my fanny all day."

"I don't exercise on the job either," noted Jack. "Do it on my own time. But it pays off."

"How? Brains alone get you power and dough and women. That's all there is."

"The Greeks said mind and body. You can't beat that combination."

"Sure," said Bill. "Look where it got the Greeks. They were swamped by the Romans and today they're an eighth-rate nation. All pat equations sound good, like two and two equal four. But in the practical world they sometimes equal three, so where are you?"

"In the locker room," said Jack.

"I should be in a whore house. What's the use of taking off my clothes here."

They laughed and Bill punched him lightly on the arm. "Muscleman," he said. In the main gymnasium they joined a class performing calisthenics to recorded music and instructions.

They waited their turn at the punching bag in the boxing room and then descended to the weight-lifting room.

"I never make progress." Bill groaned as he pushed an 80-pound barbell over his head in a military press.

Jack set up another bar with 140 pounds for the same lift. "Come with me twice a week, every week, and I'll guarantee it."

"Too much like work," replied Bill. "Always the same thing."

"But that's life – a series of repetitions. Vary it from time to time, but it boils down to exercise we repeat every day."

"Dull enough as is," said Bill. "Why add more?"

"For me it's different," began Jack. "Maybe I've been covering politicians all day and I've got double talk coming out of both ears and a headache. I think, the last thing I want to do now is lift weights. But I start in, out of habit really, and before long a wonderful thing happens – the whole damn day drops away, like a dead weight. My head clears, my blood quickens; I'm alive again."

He inhaled deeply and rested one foot on the barbell.

"Or maybe my boss has balled me out or some deskman made a stink because I left out a politician's middle initial. I'd like to smash somebody. But I can't flatten the boss or the deskman and I don't want to take it out on some innocent Joe. So I come here and pound that punching bag. I pound and pound and maybe I say to myself, 'that's for you, you petty low son-of-a-bitch.' After awhile I feel better. I can eat a thick steak and not get cramps afterward."

He walked away and selected several iron plates for a new exercise.

"That's my boy who said that," shouted Bill.

So often it was like that. You tried to talk straight from the heart, to explain something that was important to you. And the response was a wisecrack. Even from your best friend. Perhaps he had embarrassed Bill, made him feel defensive. Everybody talked in circles as if they were afraid to come to grips with things. People held back as if they feared they would slobber if they ever let go. You did not remove your shirt in public. Or did you ever?

"Smile when you say that." People smiled a lot these days, but few seemed happy.

When they left Bill suggested they go to one of the dance halls on 86th street. "Some of the foreign dames there are easy makes," he noted.

"We've got a party tomorrow night," said Jack.

"That's tomorrow night. Maybe we can pick up something for tonight."

"Join you for a quick beer," said Jack. "But I leave you the pleasure of the easy makes."

Chapter 4

A feminine laugh like a broken string of beads wafted through the open door, framed by the tinkling of glass, the chattering of casual conversations and the subdued rhythm of the cha-cha-cha.

"Nice to meet you," said Ann, pumping Bill's hand. "Drinks are in the kitchen. See you later." She squeezed Jack's fingers and whirled away so that her salmon-pink dress ballooned.

In the narrow kitchenette they found several open whiskey bottles on the sink stand guarded by a bucket of ice cubes, sodas, and an assortment of glasses. A couple embraced, leaning against the refrigerator, apparently oblivious to the world; the girl balanced a half-empty drink in one hand as her arms surrounded her partner's neck.

"Magnificent," commented Bill, pouring a bourbon and water and plopping an ice cube into the mixture. Jack filled a glass with ginger ale. For a moment they quietly observed the couple; then they re-entered the living room.

On a ruby red sofa Bill spotted a chesty blonde slowly thumbing a fashion magazine. His glance sped from her white spike-heeled shoes up her trim bare legs, her curvy hips modeled in a lavender silk dress cut revealingly low in front, to her round doll face and piled-high hair. He nudged Jack in the ribs and then plopped beside her.

"Have as much trouble as I did finding this place?"

"How much did you have?" she replied without looking away from her magazine. Bill hesitated, swigged his drink, and began to fabricate a tale of faulty directions and wrong turns in the winding byways of Greenwich Village.

Jack ambled to the phonograph and began sifting a pile of discs, casually noting the titles and bands until Ann appeared and, without a word, pulled him by the sleeve to a group in a corner.

"Want you all to meet Jack Stopple, one of the top reporters for Intercontinental News," she announced. Jack shook several hands, muttering that Ann "exaggerated a bit."

"I always wanted to go into journalism," said a heavyweight whose black pompadoured hair was like a wave about to descend on his forehead. "But somehow I drifted into law, and there I am."

"Where?" asked somebody.

"With Williams, Williams, Williams and Ginsberg," he replied, blowing a puff of smoke from a cigarette he held in a pudgy holder.

"That's a lot of Williamses for one Ginsberg," said another.

"Actually, they're all Ginsbergs who've changed their names," the lawyer said, "all except the one who held out."

"Reporting must be exciting," said a dark-haired girl beside the lawyer, "and seeing your byline in the papers all the time."

"Oh, one gets used to everything," said someone. "Isn't that so?"

"Of course," said Jack. They chatted about jobs, then shifted to psychology and then politics. Finally the group scattered and Jack drifted back to the phonograph records.

"I always know where to find you," said Ann. "Having fun?"

"Sure. Great party."

"You're shy, aren't you? Never thought of that. A big lug like you and you're shy." She rested her hand on his.

"Unhand my girl Stopple. I don't care how brawny you are, you can't steal my dearest child." Stan Cowels stood unsmiling before them, a scarlet scarf protruding from his black sweater.

Jack smiled. "Do you sleep in a sweater?"

"I'm comfortable in a sweater Stopple. I've broken forever with your gray flannel shibboleths. Besides, Ann is drawn to it. Look, she's weakening under its spell."

"You mean smell. What am I going to do with this guy Jack? He haunts me, pinches me, crashes my parties…."

"Give in, my darling," said Cowels. "We're star crossed lovers, don't you know." He closed his eyes.

"Our paths have crossed
Out in space
Our hearts were lost
In celestial embrace."

"Very pretty." She laughed. "Excuse me fellas, I want to see if the liquor's holding out." She left.

"Did you bring the chianti?" asked Jack.

"Stopple, I'm a man of my word. You know that. Can't decide whether to hate you or pity you."

Jack laughed. "Why do either?"

"Your smugness irritates me. Or perhaps it reminds me of something I want to forget. Double double toil and trouble. Beware of the ides of March. Beware, Stopple. Beware…." He walked off toward the kitchenette.

"Wait a minute Shakespeare," shouted Jack. But Cowels did not turn back and Jack decided against pursuing him. He swung back toward the phonograph and bumped a girl, spilling his ginger ale on her dress.

"You again! Clumsy oaf."

"Oh pardon me," said Jack. Instinctively he brushed some liquid from her dress.

"Don't touch me," she said, pushing his hand away. She stalked off.

Amazing that he should be thrown against this girl again, as if he were some ordained instrument sent to plague her. It was pure chance, of course, that twice in two days they had collided. But coincidence or not he owed her a formal apology. She was alone on the other side of the room, walking in a tiny circle like a furious cat.

"I'm truly sorry," he said. "I want to apologize about spilling the drink, and also about yesterday morning in the office."

"Thank you very much," she snapped. "Very considerate of you. Yesterday you seemed to think it was a big joke. But I suppose knocking people over is part of a reporter's routine; you train especially for that, don't you?"

"I assure you it was an accident – both times. And I'm truly sorry. I went back to find you yesterday – I was late for work – but you were gone." Jack waited a moment for a reply, then he continued, "how did you know I train, or did you guess?"

"I know all about you," she said.

"Not all, I hope."

"No." Then she smiled too. "Ann said you were a health enthusiast."

"Is that why you wanted to meet me?" He was sorry as soon as the words slipped out.

"Did Ann say that?"

"Not exactly. She said there was a girl interested in the same things I am." Her eyes disconcerted him: he could not concentrate on the conversation.

"I did say I wanted to meet you. Does that disturb you?"

"No. Why should it?" Of course she disturbed him; he felt she willed it so. They were on a towering fence going in opposite directions and only one could pass.

"Good," she said. "But I notice you're drinking. Does that fit your ideas on health?"

"It's only ginger ale," he explained. "Something to hold in my hand so the others don't think I'm a square. Smell if you don't believe me." He lifted his cup but she shook her head and he lowered it.

"I believe you. My name is Sylvia Parker. I'm in public relations with Atkins and Holton. Been to I.N. several times but yesterday was the first time I bumped into you."

They laughed. "We did it right, didn't we?" noted Jack. Then he introduced himself. "I'm on assignment most of the time. Guess that's why you missed me before."

She did not reply, but instead half-turned and looked around, as if suddenly bored and wanting to leave or be rescued. Well, she could go, Jack thought. I made my apology; I won't chase her. But as she twittered nervously, like a bird about to take flight, he studied her. Her skin was very white and shiny like ivory; it set off her sculptured face, her small nose with a slight hook at its center, her jet black hair cut short, her lips, thin and delicate. But her eyes dominated her face, like hazel nuts enlarged by dark pencil shadows, clear, almost liquid, like a pool seen from the high diving board.

"What is your interest in health?" she asked suddenly, her thinly penciled eyebrows arching.

"Nothing special. I exercise regularly: lift weights, run, watch my diet, don't smoke or drink, except for an occasional beer. That's about it. And you?"

"I do smoke and drink, eat whatever I like, hate exercise, can't lift an abridged dictionary and couldn't catch a train if my life depended on it."

"Seriously," she continued, "I'm writing publicity on the importance of body-building to good health. One of our accounts is the Jeff Hanford Gyms. Know them?"

"They mix indirect lighting and soft music with sweat and high-pressure salesmanship, don't they?"

"Are you a dissatisfied customer?"

"Just what I've heard. I hope you don't take it personally."

"Why should I? It's only my job."

Bill and the blonde he had approached earlier rumbaed nearby and he called out, "it's so lonely on the dance floor; keep us company." Jack and Sylvia exchanged glances and without speaking, he took her about the waist. Her lithe body glided effortlessly under his gentlest pressure, as if she could anticipate his movements.

"You must be more athletic than you admit," said Jack. "You dance extremely well."

She smiled. "You're a good leader."

When the music stopped Jack introduced Bill to Sylvia and he discovered that the blonde, Marsha Golden, shared her apartment.

"Almost makes us a family," exclaimed Marsha.

"Right," agreed Bill. "And you're the baby bear." He patted her cheek.

Ann approached, followed by Cowels. "So you found each other," she said to Jack and Sylvia. "Well, I kept my word."

"We had met before," Sylvia noted dryly.

"And who are you fair damsel of the golden tresses?" asked Cowels.

"I'm fair Marsha Golden. I teach school."

"Of course you do, dear child. Prodding our youngsters to partake of life's problems. Perhaps you teach my sons. Do you teach junior high?"

"No: fifth grade at P.S. 91. Do you have sons? How unusual"

"What's so unusual about that," said Bill. "Happens in the best of families. Come dance with me." He pulled her toward the open space in the center of the living room, but she resisted.

"No, not now silly. Everybody's talking now."

"Yes, let's dance," said Ann. "You easterners don't know how to dance; let's show them Jack." She took his hand. Bill grabbed Marsha.

"No thanks," Sylvia replied to Cowels, and she walked into the kitchenette.

"Do you like her?" asked Ann, as they danced.

"Sure. Why not?"

"I don't. Not especially. She's not your type anyway."

"You said that once before. What's my type? I've never been able to decide."

"Jack Stopple you're … exasperating." She pressed her head against his cheek. It made him uncomfortable; he did not pull away but he was happy when the music stopped.

"I've got to leave," he said, noting the midnight hour.

"Tomorrow's a workday and besides I'm doing roadwork."

"Are you in construction?" asked Marsha.

He explained that by roadwork he meant running to keep in shape and increase his wind capacity.

Have you been doing that long?" called Marsha.

"About eight years."

"You must be winded by now," she said seriously.

Bill burst into laughter; the others smiled. Jack offered to drive them home but they declined.

"Entertainment's coming," said Marsha. "Ann's lined up some Broadway talent."

Jack said goodbye. On his way to the door he noticed Sylvia conversing with a short fellow with heavy rimmed eyeglasses. He halted before them.

"Glad to have met you Miss Parker. Hope to see you again."

"Will you take me home?" she asked.

"Sure."

"I'll get my bag." She walked into the next room. The fellow with the eyeglasses edged away.

At that moment there was a burst of noise at the front door.

"Ann Rawley, baby doll, how are you?" Mark Larson had arrived, dressed in a white dinner jacket, leading two tall young women in flashy evening gowns. A man with a guitar lagged behind.

"Told you I'd come," said Larson, hugging Ann. "Your dad wrote me you were in town. Sorry I couldn't make it sooner. Ann, I want to meet Erica Dawn. She's at the Bongo Room, as if everybody didn't know. And this is Looka Lily, belly dancer supreme. Can't stay long, Ann dear. Got to get these girls back." Then he announced, "Quiet down everybody and make a circle."

The man with the guitar began tuning his instrument. The people cleared space in the living room as Sylvia walked through.

"Are you going?" Ann asked.

"There's going to be a show," Larson said; then he added, "yes. Come back."

The room was hushed as Jack opened the front door. "Seen the show?" shouted Larson. "Okay, go ahead. Walk out. But I never forget a back."

They hesitated a moment.

"If you gotta go you gotta go," taunted Larson.

Jack's breath was coming fast and he felt his arms stiffen. He nudged Sylvia brusquely out the door and followed.

"Damned showoff," muttered Jack.

"Who was he?" asked Sylvia.

"Didn't you recognize the kisser. Mark Larson. Mark Larson, renowned television personality."

"Yes, now that you mention it. Should we go back?"

"Not me, hell no." He halted at the bottom of the stairs. "Are you coming?"

"Yes," she said.

When they arrived on upper Riverside Drive she invited him in for coffee. He accepted, but requested tea.

"No got," she said. They compromised on beer. "Not much food available, either. Want some cookies?"

"Whatever you have will be fine," he replied. She went into the kitchen and Jack sat on a tan foam rubber sofa. The living room had a blond portable television set, an automatic phonograph, a small but well-stocked bookcase near a roll-top desk, and several chairs. Two abstract paintings hung on the walls.

"Did I mention I'm working on body-building copy?" she asked, returning with a tray of white crackers and an open bottle of beer with two glasses.

"I think so."

"Don't know much about it though. Could you help – read my stuff and give me a few pointers? This has got to appeal to guys with middle age spread as well as those with bulging biceps."

"Sure, glad to help. I'm no expert though."

"It's in my office now."

Jack declined a second beer. At the door he asked if he could see her again Sunday afternoon but she suggested he telephone next week.

"Best to call me at the office," she said, and gave him the telephone number. When she handed him the slip of paper he kissed her quickly on the mouth. He saw her eyes close and he kissed her again, slowly enfolding her but without pressure.

"Thanks darling," she whispered.

He swept her in his arms and kissed her neck and ear and throat and lips. Her eyes opened and she pushed him away.

"Good night," she said softly. He did not budge. "Good night love," she said and eased him out the door.

Chapter 5

At 7 a.m. the alarm clock clanged like a fire bell. Jack stretched over his head to the kitchen table, pushed down the button, and fell asleep again immediately. But an instant later he jumped up as an imaginary alarm sounded in a dream. He sped through his calisthenics, concluding with fifty pushups, washed, donned his gray sweat clothes and tennis shoes, ate an orange and jogged downstairs.

The sun blinded him like a sudden explosion. He shook his head several times to lose his dull grogginess, breathing deeply of the warm spring air. It was a lovely day, dry but with a soft breeze that fluttered the leafy green maples and elms. He trotted into Central Park, crossed the black loam horseback riding path and jumped the low three-strand wire fence that ringed the outer edge of the reservoir's cinder path. A mounted policeman waved from a distance and Jack returned his salutation.

Jack alternated between jogging and running around the mile and a half track. Responding to the exercise; his lungs filled with air, his blood tingled with tiny electric charges. Two gray seagulls perched majestically on the eight-foot wire fence that enclosed the billion gallon reservoir, their white square heads upright, their yellow beaks jerking to the left and right. As Jack approached they tip-toed along the fence in a delicate ladies walk until finally they spread their wings and flew off.

Sylvia had been so cold and unapproachable until the last moments in her apartment; then she was a pulsating woman, exciting, suddenly of flesh and blood. Had he released her true self from its slick shell? A flattering thought. Yet he wanted to believe that their violent meetings were not entirely accidental and that, in some mysterious manner, he had reached the essential woman in her. He would telephone hello later on.

At the end of his third lap he burst into speed; then he trotted to the tennis court locker rooms nearby, showered and dressed for work with clothes he stored there. He arrived downtown twenty minutes before nine and breakfasted in the I.N. building's luncheonette.

"Gentlemen," he announced to Adams and Twist, "I'm three minutes early this morning and don't want to be disturbed."

He picked up a telephone receiver and began dialing. But then he hung up. Perhaps she is still asleep, he thought. My hello won't be so welcome then. Besides, she had suggested he call next week; better not appear too eager.

"Are you available now, Captain Stopple?" asked Mr. Adams.

"At your service, Admiral."

"Good. Glad to have you aboard. Do the weather."

Jack sent the copy boy to the financial department to fetch the weather report. The teletype machine that received weather bureau information had been relocated there recently, following a new theory that storms sometime explain why one stock shoots up or another declines.

The weather bureau's abbreviations could be confusing; they employed a common sense code that often didn't make much. For example, "fr cd dur erl mrn becm cld in pm" meant "fair and cold during the early morning, becoming cloudy in the afternoon." But the same forecast might come over "fa col dr ery am bcg cly aft."

To Jack's surprise, the report for New York City and vicinity read: "erl mrn rn edg by pm, fr wrm aft & evn." This translated to "early morning rain ending by afternoon, fair and warm in the afternoon and evening." He could recall no early morning precipitation; the gravel around the reservoir had been dry. His impulse was to transcribe the report verbatim, since the weather bureau was the authority in these matters. On the other hand, the rain had presumably occurred by now, and if it hadn't, the newspapers might squawk.

"Hello, weather bureau? This is Intercontinental News. Will you go over the early forecast with me? I think there may be an error."

"In the forecast or the teletyping" asked the voice on the telephone.

"I don't know. That's what I want to check."

"We're not God you know."

"Yes, I know," replied Jack. "The forecast for New York City and vicinity reads 'early morning rain ending by afternoon'."

"You didn't read the whole thing."

"After that it says 'fair and warm in the afternoon and evening'."

"Well?"

"I don't remember any rainfall this morning," said Jack. "Was there any?

"I don't think so, but the morning isn't over yet."

"Yes, but the early morning is," insisted Jack. "It's nearly ten o'clock. The sun is shining and there's hardly a cloud in the sky."

"You've been looking out the window, haven't you?" the telephone voice asked suspiciously.

"Yes," admitted Jack.

"You know we don't calculate weather that way. You're aware of our scientific approach. I'm really surprised at you."

"I'm sorry. I didn't mean to question your techniques. But are you going to change the forecast?"

"I can't do that. Only the chief meteorologist can."

"Well, will he?" persisted Jack.

"How should I know? He's out for coffee. Besides, he seldom does. You had better run it the way it is. As I said, the morning isn't over and we haven't given up hope"

Jack hung up and explained the situation to Mr. Adams. "The clients will be screaming for the forecast any minute," he said, pulling at the remaining hairs on his head. "Send it out as is, but make sure you attribute everything to the weather bureau!"

Jack arrived 20 minutes late for his luncheon assignment at the Hotel Regina, knowing that such weekend functions invariably ran behind schedule. He strolled through the mirrored lobby, skirting the main ballroom for a small door on which had been tacked a sign, "Guests of Honor." A uniformed guard stopped him.

"Press," said Jack. The guard stepped aside.

The luncheon was being given by the New York City Association of Labor Organizations, known by the initials CALO, to honor Mayor Simpson for his pro-labor administration. Jack observed the Mayor sipping a cocktail and chatting with several labor leaders near a makeshift bar. Joe Dugan, a former newsman who was CALO's publicity director, came forward with a slim, nattily dressed man, Myron Foster, one of the Mayor's many assistants.

"You know Jack Stopple of Intercontinental News," said Dugan.

"Oh yes," said Foster. "Met often at city hall. How are you Jack?"

"Fine," said Jack, shaking his hand. He was certain he had never spoken to Foster before, though he had seen him in the city hall press room.

Foster lifted a mimeographed text from a folder. "The mayor's address," he said, handing a copy to Jack.

Across the top of the first page in bold letters was, "Not to be released before 2:30 p.m." Jack leafed the text. It seemed a rather dull recapitulation of labor's activities in the city during the Mayor's administration. But it was reassuring to have. The Mayor was one of those well-educated men whose off-the-cuff remarks were a maze of run-on misconstructed phrases. But he could usually be relied upon to follow a prepared speech.

"Pretty general stuff," noted Jack. "You write it?"

"The Mayor's rather busy this time of year," replied Foster.

The ballroom was decorated with red, white and blue bunting, the emblems of various labor unions, the CALO emblem, and city, state and national insignia. The press table, marked with a placard in black block letters, was directly in front of the elevated dais so that the view of the speakers would be like the front row of a movie. Jack sat between Dugan and Tom Castle, a reporter for the Daily Express.

Speaking softly into the microphone at the center of the dais, the Reverend J. Alexander Smyth asked the assemblage to rise for the invocation. He thanked the Lord for the plentiful food placed before his servants. Then he called upon God to bless the labor movement, singling out the national leaders of the AFL-CIO. He named the state and city labor officials, occasionally glancing down the dais to make sure he had not missed anyone. He called for Supreme Guidance for Mayor Simpson and the city administration; the governor, the lieutenant governor and the state administration. He passed on to the President of the United States, the Vice-President, the Secretary of State (and several other secretaries in the federal government), the Congress, the Supreme Court. He sat down suddenly; his audience followed suit, devouring their fruit cups.

The press table waiter had dark eyes that appeared to observe life ominously above a prominent hooked nose and a bushy black mustache, its long hairs flying wild and loose. His head was completely bald. Grimly, he demanded a luncheon ticket from each person at the table; Jack and Tom Castle lacked them. Dugan insisted that the reporters did not need them and offered to assume the responsibility. But the waiter demurred; there would be no main course without tickets. Finally, the maître d' hotel arbitrated the matter successfully.

The waiters brought out platters of chicken swimming in a heavy brown gravy. The press table waiter, balancing his tray precariously in one hand, circled about, demanding "leg or breast" and then plopping the appropriate piece into each plate. Last to be served was a thin woman, one of the union office workers. The waiter had plunked down a chicken leg and held his ladle poised to drown the morsel when she exclaimed:

"But I want a breast."

"I only got a leg lady," he said. "It's the last piece."

"I don't see why everybody should get what they ordered except me," she said, fluttering her eyelashes.

"I only got a leg lady. You don't want a leg?" He waved the gravy-loaded ladle back and forth.

"There must be more chicken in the kitchen," said Dugan. "If she wants a breast, give her a breast."

The waiter seemed to be struggling with his sanity. "Breast," he said, spitting out the word. His mustache twitched. Then he replaced the ladle in the tray, picked up the woman's plate, and marched away. He returned in five minutes with a tiny chicken breast and departed without a word.

From the dais came the tinkling of a fork striking a water glass. Jack Weingarten, vice-president of the Ladies Clothing Union, and the master of ceremonies, introduced Marie Consolo, shop steward, "who will graciously entertain us with a few musical selections." A small dark-haired woman walked with determination to the stage at the end of the dais and, accompanied by a pianist, sang "Begin the Beguine." The luncheon guests, mostly union men, continued eating and drinking the beer and whisky placed at each table. Miss Consolo edged closer to the microphone for "Oh What a Beautiful Morning" as the noise in the ballroom increased. The louder she sang the greater the general confusion. Miss Consolo had a sweet voice but her attempt to increase its volume led her off pitch. "I Like New York in June" was a battle to dominate the hall. She persevered with "Oklahoma." But the issue was in doubt until the finale; then she hugged the microphone so that it seemed she might swallow it. She sang louder and louder and when she reached the last bars she summoned the whole of her 98-odd pounds.

"I'll ne-vair walk ay-lone," she concluded. The audience knew she meant it and applauded mightily as she strode off stage.

The waiter returned with a vanilla ice cream cake on a large tray and a bowl of strawberries in a heavy sauce. His task: to slice the cake, serve it, and then smother it with strawberry sauce, all the time balancing the tray and sauce bowl in his arms. An amazing feat. A veteran of many luncheons, Jack appreciated the dexterity and style with which the waiter swept around the table. But he was aware of the dangers, too, and when the waiter served him, Jack leaned far back.

Dugan was waving instructions to the commercial photographer and neither heeded the waiter nor observed the strawberry sauce dripping onto his suit. But Jack did and so did the waiter. They exchanged penetrating glances. The waiter departed, returning soon to place a coffee pot on the table. He glared again at Jack as if to strike some sort of pact with him or perhaps hypnotise him into a state of forgetfulness. Then he sauntered away, jerking his head upward with an air of finality, as if to say, "Nothing matters now."

The gob of strawberry slid slowly into the pack of cigarettes in Dugan's lapel pocket. It dripped into the filter tips. Suddenly Dugan caught Jack's stare. "God damnit." He looked up angrily for the waiter, who by this time, was probably collecting his pay for the afternoon's work. "Did you see him do that?"

"An accident," said Jack. "You were busy."

"I ought to bill him," said Dugan, still trying to glimpse the waiter. But all the waiters had disappeared. Dungan dipped his cloth napkin into his water glass and dabbed the spot.

The tinkling of silverware against glass emanated again from the dais. But it was ignored by the audience. The master of ceremonies hit his glass harder and suddenly there was a cracking and swishing as water spilled. Several men jumped up at the main table.

"May I have your attention, PLEASE," said Mr. Weingarten, sopping up the water with his napkin.

A "ssshhhhhhhhhh" in the audience silenced all but one rear table whose occupants apparently had consumed too much whisky to care.

"If we can all settle down a bit," began Mr. Weingarten, "I would like to introduce the guests on the dais. I know they are well known to most of you, so in the interest of saving time, let there be no applause until the last person has been called. Then, all together, we can let them know what we think of them."

Beginning at his extreme right, the M.C. introduced Tom Haley, business manager of local 799, United Steamfitters, Boilermakers and Plumbers. As he arose somebody shouted, "Hooray for Haley," and two others clapped vigorously. Mr. Haley waved to them and sat down.

Pete McArthur, president of the Men's Suits and Garment Workers, drew scattered handclaps. He sat down glumly. Casey O'hara, vice-president of the Barmaids, Bartenders and Sweepers International, knocked over his chair as he got up. He retrieved it and then stood erect. A chorus of cheers and applause was led by the noisy rear table. Mr. O'hara clenched both hands over his head like a winning prizefighter, but he quickly lowered them when he noticed Mr. Weingarten's disapproving scowl. Thereafter, everybody introduced was applauded.

The first speaker was Congressman Emanuel J. Kaufmann, Bronx Democrat, a short wiry man whose bushy eyebrows fluttered to punctuate his sentences. Making the most of his lead-off position, the Congressman immediately predicted that a bill he was cosponsoring would become "the most important piece of labor legislation since the Wagner Act."

"The press, for reasons well known to all of you, has seen fit to suppress my proposed legislation or else distort its meaning," he declared. There were scattered boos.

Tom Castle whispered "He never complains when we support him at election time."

"By distortion he means somebody misspelled his name," suggested Jack.

The Congressman read long excerpts from his proposal to reorganize the National Labor Relations Board. Labor disputes leading to strikes could be drastically reduced, he declared, by making employers financially responsible for wages lost by striking workers if the N.L.R.B. ruled in favor of the union. He cited other proposed regulations for employers, skimming over his plans to curb labor. This aspect of his bill had been emphasized last week in his talk before the County Chamber of Commerce.

"… and the rights of labor will be safeguarded and protected as long as I have a voice in Congress," he concluded.

Mr. Weingarten took the microphone as the applause subsided. "Our next speaker needs no introduction," he said, "our own Maxwell J. Farnsworth." The audience cheered loudly.

"From the day he was born Max Farnsworth has had the interests of labor foremost in his heart," the M.C. continued. He traced Farnsworth's life from the cradle "up the ranks of labor" to the CALO presidency.

Jack's notes on the Congressman amounted to less than a page. His bill had been thoroughly reported from Washington. Now Jack started a clean page in his notebook and headed it, "Farnsworth – 1." But the CALO president apparently had decided to be brief and thereby spotlight the Mayor. Farnsworth was among friends and without a burning issue, so he spoke in generalities, letting his deep and resonant voice linger melodiously upon the "rightful goals of labor" and occasionally turn raspy and harsh during a condemnation of "Big Business" and "strike-breakers." Approaching the end, he turned on his vocal power.

"… the forces in this city that would turn back the clock, that would restrict the labor movement, that would hamstring us, the forces that would put us back into the chains that we fought so voluminously to break.."

Jack peered swiftly at Castle's notes to see if he had caught the last words correctly. But Farnsworth continued.

"… when labor had its back to the wall, when the city administration was hostile to the aims and rightful ambitions of the working people, when the police were a tool of the bosses, as in many cities and towns in America they still are, they will not succeed, they must not succeed...."

Farnsworth paused as if out of breath. Then in a hoarse whisper that rose in pitch and intensity with each syllable until it ended in a shout, he declared, "they must be de-FEAT-ED!"

Only Jack and Castle remained seated as the audience responded.

The Mayor stuck to the text. Speaking in a quavering monotone, he traced labor's relations with the city over the years, emphasizing the legislative acts and executive decisions during his reign which had "strengthened labor's bargaining position." He paused several times for polite applause. When he had finished the prepared address the audience response was rather mild. Mayor Simpson wiped his brow and leaned against the dais.

"As long as I am Mayor, New York will be a labor town," he shouted. That clinched it; a three-minute standing ovation followed. Then Mr. Farnsworth began, "For He's a Jolly Good Fellow," and the song was quickly taken up by the ballroom.

"Not much of a story," said Jack on the way out.

"Usual crap," said Castle. "But you never can tell what the office will want. It's been a slow day."

Jack telephoned his office and said he had only a few paragraphs to give in. "The speakers either repeated old stuff or spoke in vague generalities," he said.

"Are you off your rocker?" boomed Mr. Adams. "You had a congressman, the mayor and the labor boss of this town."

"I know, I know," replied Jack. "But they didn't say a damn thing. There isn't even a solid lead."

"They must have said something," barked Mr. Adams. "You've been there all afternoon. Two papers called for the story and I promised at least 700 words. So let's have it Stopple. Use your imagination."

"For 700 words I'll have to describe the wallpaper."

"Shove the wallpaper, Stopple. Lead with the Mayor and make it good."

Jack hesitated; for a moment he felt like slamming down the receiver. But Mr. Adams voice snapped him out of it. "Are you ready, Stopple? What's happened to you? I'm switching you to rewrite."

"Okay, okay." Jack reread his notes as the telephone operator switched the call. Then he dictated:

"Mayor Simpson promised nearly 1,000 cheering union workers today that New York would remain a labor stronghold as long as he continues as its chief.

"As long as I am Mayor, New York will be a labor town," he declared.

"The mayor was the guest of honor at a luncheon in the Hotel Regina sponsored by the New York City Association of Labor Organizations. He received a three-minute standing ovation at the conclusion of his address.

"Sharing the platform was Maxwell J. Farnsworth, CALO president, who lashed out at those who, he said, "would thwart labor's rightful goals…""

The next day the "Express" carried Castle's bylined story on page one. It quoted liberally from the Mayor's text. The other newspapers also displayed the story prominently, using Jack's wire service copy verbatim or editing it slightly; every newspaper carried the byline of its own reporter specializing in politics.

Chapter 6

Jack reclined in a swivel chair, his feet propped on a waste basket, reading a tabloid when Sylvia telephoned.

"How've you been?" she asked.

"Fine. I meant to call you tonight."

"You promised to help with my body-building copy. I'm holding you to it."

"Yes. I want to. Any time you say."

"What about tonight?" she suggested. "Say, eight o'clock at my place."

"Tuesdays I usually exercise at the Y," he thought aloud,

"How about afterward? We could make it later."

"Okay. About nine."

"I'll be expecting you. Bye." She clicked off.

Mr. Adams tipped up his eyeshade. "Are you finished with your personal calls Mr. Stopple?" He added, "blonde or brunette?"

"Never touch the stuff," said Jack. "What can you do for me?"

"Listen." Mr. Adams pointed with his index finger.

"Go over to 39th street and Madison Avenue. Know the Consolidated International building going up there?"

"I've seen it. Nearly finished."

"Right. Well, there are pigeons trapped inside. They're trying to rescue them."

Jack rolled down his sleeves and reached for his jacket.

"Construction workers?"

"No, no. You heard me. I said pigeons. Pigeons. You know. Ever discovered one parked over your head?"

"Since when do we cover pigeons?"

"Since now. Take a look. See what you can do."

The 65-floor aluminum and glass sheathed structure gleamed in the sunlight, a monument to man's prowess. It would rob the people of air and light and add to the congestion and already overwhelming traffic problems. Within its slick exterior would breed nervous stomachs and ulcers; a place where elevator men would gray prematurely. But still it was a wonder and a tribute, the steel beams rising from gigantic craters in the earth, the huge derricks and cranes, the hundreds of workmen assisting in the grinding noisy dusty metallic birth.

"I'm with Intercontinental News," Jack told the guard at the wire fence surrounding the building. "I understand you've got some … things trapped inside."

"Got identification?" It was one of the rare times he had to show his police department press card.

"Okay." The guard smiled. "You'll find the rest of them on the second floor. Take the escalator." He pointed the direction.

"The rest of them," to Jack's amazement, turned out to be three reporters and five photographers. Also, a dozen construction workers, a press agent and a bespectacled representative of the American Society for the Prevention of Cruelty to Animals.

Another reporter explained, "These pigeons, see, they made roost in the beams while the building was going up. Now the place is walled in and they're hidden up in the spaces afraid to come out."

"So what?" demanded Jack. "Don't they always get caught in new constructions?"

"Don't ask me," he replied. "I go where I'm sent."

Two refreshment stands had been set up on the huge bare floor which still lacked office partitions. Behind one, a girl in white cap and apron served coffee and pastry; the other table, supervised by a uniformed bartender, contained several whiskies, a tray of glasses and a bucket of ice cubes.

"No point in being thirsty if we have to wait," said the press agent nervously. His scheme had worked brilliantly: the large turnout meant sure publicity for the building. Perhaps his timing had been perfect; his call to city editors coming at a dull moment. But Jack did not rule out connections between the building sponsors, the publicity agency, and the news executives.

The reporters and photographers circulated between the bar and the coffee table, encouraged by the press agent who apparently feared some might leave. Meanwhile, construction workers scoured for pigeons. The ASPCA agent neither ate nor drank. Like a hunter, intent and determined, he paced noiselessly near an opening in the ceiling, his net and several extension poles in hand.

Suddenly somebody shouted that a pigeon was loose on the 57th floor. "Let's go," said the press agent. "Don't worry about your drinks. We'll keep the bar open." He led the way to a small service elevator; the main elevators were not yet operating. Only half the party could fit in; the others had to wait for the vehicle to descend.

"Don't catch anything 'till we get there," yelled a photographer.

The view from the 57th floor was a breathtaking panorama of the city. Jack could see the East River and Queens and west to the Hudson river and Hoboken and farther south the flatlands of New Jersey. But there was no time for gazing, for, strutting on the floor was a dusty gray pigeon, the greenish shine about its neck dulled perhaps by confinement. The ASPCA man attached extension poles to his net and tip-toed forward, heeled by the photographers and reporters who emulated his walk. Then came the press agent and several construction workers like a darkening cloud.

Abruptly the bird took wing; it flew close to the 15-foot ceiling, making small circles and fluttering its wings madly. The

ASPCA man prepared to swing his net when suddenly the pigeon made for the far side of the room. Swoooooosh went the net, just missing the bird as the cameras flashed.

The bird flew nearly the distance of a street, with the men in pursuit. The ASPCA man waved the others back but nobody wanted to miss the catch. The panicky bird flew down another corridor and the ASPCA man slowed his pace, apparently trying to pacify his prey. But the clacking newsmen and photographers lugging their cameras and cases of flashbulbs and other paraphernalia dissipated his caution.

Unexpectedly, the pigeon tried to retrace its path over the heads of the throng. Perceiving his opportunity, the agent swung upward in a great arc, netting the frightened creature. He lowered the net to the floor and removed the pigeon with his hand.

"We didn't get a picture." "It happened too fast." "Why didn't you warn us?"

A photographer demanded that he release the bird and catch it again. The ASPCA man refused. "These guys need a picture," pleaded the press agent. But the ASPCA man was adamant. It would be unnecessarily cruel, he insisted, adding significantly that he might be unable to recapture it. Grumbling, the photographers snapped the pigeon in the agent's hand.

At this moment word was received that another pigeon was loose on the second floor.

"Another chance," chorused the photographers. "And near the bar," added the press agent. Everyone rushed for the elevator.

When they reached the second floor they found Mark Larson there with his television crew.

"I'll need a tight shot of the capture," he told the press agent. "Where shall I set up my equipment?"

The press agent beckoned the ASPCA man who, meanwhile, had plugged the hole in the ceiling from which the pigeon had escaped. "I can't tell where I'll catch it or even if I will," he said.

"I sympathize," said Larson, adjusting his tie to the collar of his pale blue shirt. "But consider the viewers – millions waiting to see you in action, pulling for you to succeed."

"The whole country will be rooting for you," added the press agent, ecstatic at the prospect of television coverage.

The ASPCA man said he would try to maneuver the bird into the northwest corner of the floor. "But I can't promise it," he added.

The television crew placed their kleiglights and cameras in the northwest corner. A microphone was set up on a pile of wooden boards and a chair with MARK LARSON printed on back was unfolded next to the microphone. The ASPCA man, who had been told to wait until the TV crew finished, nervously watched the crew and the fluttering pigeon. Larson called him. "We'll need a dry run now, Mr. ...."

"Johnson," volunteered the ASPCA man. "Sam Johnson."

"Now, Mr. Johnson," said Larson, "speak directly into the microphone and tell the viewers how it feels to have caught this pigeon."

"I didn't catch it yet."

"I know." Larson grinned tightly. "This is only a voice test."

The photographers and reporters grumbled at the delay. "We can't wait," said Jack to the press agent, but loud enough for Larson to overhear. The press agent spoke confidentially to Larson.

"All right," said the television commentator. "Always try to please. We'll do the run through later." His eyes narrowed for an instant on Jack; then he smiled broadly. "On with the show."

As if also under the spell of television direction, the pigeon had flown into the northwest corner. To insure it remaining there, the press agent ordered construction workers to hold wooden planks high, walling in the area. On a nod from Larson the press agent nudged Mr. Johnson, The ASPCA man stepped gingerly and raised his net. Suddenly the klieg lights flooded everything bright white. Mr. Johnson froze but the bird, obviously not stage struck, made for the shadows. The pigeon's movement snapped Mr. Johnson alive and, swinging with the deftness of a tennis champion making an overhead smash, he netted the bird. This time the photographers were ready and all had shots of the capture. Later they snapped Mr. Johnson staring into the pigeon's orange eye. This posed shot, reflecting a certain rapport between man and bird, rather than the action picture, appeared next day in most newspapers.

The reporters interviewed Mr. Johnson quickly, determining his age, his family, his service with the animal agency. He said he had made many such captures; the pigeons would be released later in Central Park. Then they followed the photographers out, leaving him to be interviewed on tape for television.

"Looks like this town has a new hero," said the press agent cheerfully.

Chapter 7

That evening Jack cut his gym routine to six weight lifting exercises and, after a snack in the Y cafeteria, drove to Riverside Drive. He circled until a parked car's headlights flashed on and quickly backed into the vacated space. The huge apartment house had an elevator for each half and Jack hesitated in the lobby, unable to recall which he had taken before. His guess proved correct.

"Sorry I'm late," he said as Sylvia opened the door.

"I know," she replied. "Parking problems."

She led the way into the living room. "You remember Marsha." Her roommate, in tight-fitting dungarees and a white blouse open at the neck, was stretched on the sofa.

"Hi. I'm the windy one."

"I'm concentrating on nothing," said Marsha, remaining supine. "I'm concentrating on nothing."

"Phonograph stuck?" asked Jack, smiling. Sylvia explained that her roommate practiced mental exercises.

"I have passed into nothingness," said Marsha in her flat nasal voice. She sat up suddenly. "I am not wanted here so I will pass into nothingness in the next room."

"Don't go on my account," insisted Jack. "I'd like to learn something about nothing."

"Maybe you will," she said inscrutably. "By the way, I have a date with your pal Bill Friday night. Why don't you two come along?"

"Good idea." Jack thought she wiggled purposely as she left. "Have fun," she said, closing the door behind her.

She's very original," said Sylvia sarcastically.

She invited him to sit beside her on the sofa, but she got up immediately. "Want a drink?"

"Carrot juice," he replied, "on the rocks please."

"Settle for pineapple?" He said yes and she fetched two small glasses. "Did I tell you Atkins and Holton want to make the country health conscious? We're doing it for the Jeff H. Gyms."

"Very public spirited," said Jack.

"Exactly. There's a national defense angle. We're stressing exercise."

"I can tell you where the muscles are and how to develop them," he offered.

"Trouble is, we can't be technical. At a brainstorming session we decided the public is bored by details. So we implant the idea that good health is attainable without fuss,"

He laughed softly. "It's your baby."

"Just a minute. I'll show you," She went into another room. When she returned with two typewritten pages there was a hint of hyacinth in the air. She sat beside him and read aloud:

"Americans are learning these days that the secrets of good health are not to be found only in vitamin pills or special diets. The body needs exercise to keep its vigor and make one feel truly alive and ready for the challenges of the modern world. Exercise in our modern era doesn't mean hard work. Today and everyday, millions of Americans who come to the Jeff H. Gyms learn that exercise can be fun."

Jack interrupted, "it can be hard work too."

"Not the Jeff H. way." She smiled and continued:

"People used to think that exercise was merely a way to lose weight. But scientific research discovered that the body's weight loss was insignificant compared with the gain in strength and vitality. Though your weight might not diminish, it did become more meaningful on your body. The exercised body becomes firm instead of flabby.

"Long ago, Jeff Hanford learned the secrets of successful, painless exercise. He developed the Jeff H. method. Now in Jeff H. Gyms throughout the country, you, too, can learn the pleasures of healthy living….."

Jack followed the swift movements of her lips, Her copy seemed adequate; it had a familiar ring, as if with only slight alterations it would sell soap chips as well as exercise. But she fascinated him, stiffly erect, her eyes focused on the sheets of paper in her tapered fingers; her nervous intensity like a flame whose heat attracted him and yet called upon him for protection.

"… the Jeff H. gymnasiums provide…."

He imagined her suddenly with bulging hips, a heavy sagging bust and flabby thighs, groaning as she performed deep knee bends to the cha-cha-cha; then she was in a thickly carpeted boudoir doing sit-ups with a dumbbell behind her neck, gritting a smile of feigned enjoyment.

"It wasn't that funny," she said.

"No, no, not at all. I thought of something else." He assumed a serious mien. "Of course you oversimplify the case for exercise. It's not as much fun as you make it seem."

"But you must enjoy it," she said, "or you wouldn't do it."

"That doesn't necessarily follow." He became attentive to her reasoning. "I don't enjoy getting up early. And running or lifting weights takes real effort and concentration."

"Then why do it?" she persisted.

"For the results. I feel better for it. More alive. That's my reward. If I neglect my routines I get sluggish, sometimes depressed. So I start up again."

"In other words," she said, "the ends justify the means." He smiled. "That sounds grim. I look on exercise as a sound investment. I'd buy the stock of a company that makes fighter planes or guided missiles if I believed circumstances would favor it. But that doesn't mean I have to become a warmonger."

He settled back into the softness of the cushions. "Exercise is like work. I imagine few people enjoy work; they hold jobs to earn money to do other things. What people really enjoy is seldom profitable. So you put in your nine-to-five; or in my case, nine-to-six – the lunch hour's on us."

A faucet dripped like the ticking of a clock.

"Funny that a reporter should talk that way," she mused.

"Getting around as you do, meeting new people all the time, a witness to all that's exciting and different, I'd think that the most enjoyable life imaginable."

"Well it is," he insisted. "I suppose it is. Actually, I haven't given it much thought. I enjoy my work, usually; it's not as exciting as many think. But then, nothing is when you're at it day in and day out. Still I'd rather be reporting than anything else."

But when he had said it he was uneasy, as if something had been neglected.

"In my job I'm limited by my product," said Sylvia. "I've got to stay with it, even when it begins to bore me. But with news the challenge is always there, isn't it? You're always creating. If you don't report the news, it's as if it never happened. Like the tree that falls unseen in the forest. You breathe life into the world."

"But only the breath, or the illusion of the breath." He wiped his hands along his trousers and turned to face her. "Every newsman tries to be honest. No matter how cynically he talks, deep down he wants to tell the truth."

"Doesn't he?" she asked.

He took her hands in his, feeling warmth infuse his body. Would she help him understand, would she have the patience to bear him try to put into words what he was unsure of?

"So much of our work is spreading the words of others. Politicians, civic leaders, officials of labor and business. In idealistic speeches, fighting speeches, they promise people a better life. They say they will strike down injustice and corruption. In beautiful clear sometimes poetic prose they talk of peace and prosperity and equality and justice.

"Well, we newsmen know that the speech was probably ghosted by a professional and that the politician may have only received his copy a few moments before he delivered it. Being closer to these so-called leaders than the public we're sometimes aware of a gigantic hoax. But to be objective, to be impartial, to be true to our own code of honor, we've got to report the speech as it was given. If the man condemns graft and corruption, we must report it that way, even if we know him to be a fraud, even if we have reason to believe he's involved in the very corruption he's condemning.

"The reporter's job is to tell what happened. He can be graphic, even picturesque, but he's supposed to keep himself out of the story. His very objectivity often helps to create false hopes and illusions and make giants out of shadows."

Jack clasped her hands tighter and noticed her wince; he released her. "Only today I made a hero out of a guy who caught a pigeon. It was a publicity stunt and I knew it and every reporter and photographer and editor knew it. I played the story cute; I had to do something with it. Maybe it was harmless entertainment. Probably the International Consolidated building will get rented with or without publicity."

He paused but Sylvia said nothing.

"The reporter toys with life," he continued. "No matter how much he thinks he's digging into a subject – and there's seldom time for that – he's essentially on the surface, always, playing with facts and truth like unrelated bits of driftwood."

He sighed, feeling suddenly exhausted and a little dizzy.

"I shouldn't cavil. I don't usually. I don't know how I started but thanks for listening. You're a damn good listener."

She smiled. "What the world really needs is exercise," she said.

Her parted lips dared him and swiftly he kissed them, softly, affectionately. He closed his eyes and let himself drift off into a blissful void.

"Still remember my article?" she asked, breaking away finally.

"Yes. It was fine." Then he added, "have you exercised much?"

She shook her head, swishing her hair. "At school I cut my gym class."

"If you want to gain perspective, you should."

"Won't I lose my objectivity?"

"You won't lose anything," he replied, "not even weight."

They grinned. "What should I do?" She asked.

"Run around the reservoir with me tomorrow morning."

"Oh, there must be something less strenuous."

"You see," he exclaimed in mock triumph. "You're really not interested in being creative. Are you afraid? How can you write effectively if you don't test your ideas?"

"All right, you win. I'm not afraid, Jack, you really don't know me."

"Good enough. I'll be here at 7 a.m. Sharp. Be ready."

He left soon afterward. When the front door slammed Marsha came out of her room. "How did it go?" she asked.

"He's nice," said Sylvia. "A little mixed up though."

"As usual," said Marsha.

Sylvia began laughing to herself. "Oh, this is going to be fun." The laughter escaped her throat.

"What's so amusing about Jack Stopple, the all-American boy?"

"You don't know all," said Sylvia. "I've agreed to exercise. Tomorrow Jackie and I will run in Central Park – at seven in the morning!"

Marsha shook her head. "Why do you go for athletic types? That racing car idiot almost killed you; you were lucky to escape with only a scar on your face. Then there was that jiu-jitsu fiend who even tried to throw me once. And now a hundred yard dash man. Really, kid, what are you looking for?"

"Nothing, really." Sylvia shrugged. "Or maybe everything. What's wrong with just living. These guys have ideas; they're doing things. Why shouldn't I play along. Just because they're a little crazy. Aren't we all, a little?"

"But it's just wear and tear, honey," said Marsha. "In the long run you are nowhere."

"Oh, phooey on the long run. And on your practical mind. In the long run we'll all be in the same place – six feet below the earth."

Sylvia's eyes narrowed as she looked away; a corner of her mouth twisted upward. "I saw my mother buried. I saw them lower the casket and then shovel dirt over it. Shoveling dirt over her; that was the final insult. I cried my heart out on that field of stones and crosses. You know why? Not because she was dead. She'd been dead most of her life, marrying at seventeen and raising eight kids with my stupid father, the biggest baby in the family. I cried for the shame of it. For the terrible waste of her sweet precious life. Drudgery and heartache and for what? She believed in heaven and for her sake I hope there is one because there she'll get her reward. But not me. I'm not depending on the next world. They threw dirt over her sweet body; she who had never thought of herself for a minute, who had always given of herself to whoever asked….."

She turned on Marsha angrily with tears clouding her eyes. "Well that's not for me. I'll take my life right now, if you please. I want my kicks right here, and where I find them. I'll give, but I'll take my share too. And nobody makes a fool of me, no matter what you think."

"All right, honey, take it easy," said Marsha soothingly. "I didn't mean to offend you. I'm sorry if it sounded that way."

Sylvia smiled grimly and wiped her eyes. "I know. You're only looking out for me, you would-be mother of infants." She hugged Marsha quickly. "Anyway, you can set your mind at ease as far as Jack is concerned. I've a very practical interest in him. The Hanford account is my break at Atkins and Holton, and Jack can help me with his press connection."

"But will he?" asked Marsha.

"He will. Even if I have to do a hundred laps around Central Park."

"Is that all you're prepared to do?" her roommate asked slyly.

"Why Marsha Golden, whatever do you mean?" mocked Sylvia.

Chapter 8

A brawny brown bear fled up Park Avenue. Sylvia pursued, brandishing a coiled whip. Behind her were a swarm of antique automobiles. The animal slowed and Sylvia cracked her whip over its head; it ran faster. The cars, ancient and rickety, closed in; suddenly one leaped ahead of the traffic. The driver, in a white helmet and thick sunglasses, stuck his head out the window and shouted, "let him beat you." The heads of the other drivers popped out of their vehicles. "Yes yes, yes yes, yes yes," they chanted. She lashed at the cars and they blew their horns. The sound was strained and piercing, like that of a shophar. "That's against the law," she shouted. But the horns grew louder; they took on a ringing sound...."

Startled, Sylvia set up in bed and pressed her hands against her ears. Then she turned off the alarm. The room was dark but the luminescent dial read 6:25 a.m. She slipped into her houseshoes and pulled the cord of the venetian blinds. The pale light of morning filtered through, throwing shadows of bars across the far wall. She groped in her closet for slacks and sports clothes, fishing them out piece by piece and flinging them on the bed.

She dressed, washed quickly and was boiling water for instant coffee when she noticed her high heels. She tossed them into an overnight bag she had filled with clothes for the office and changed to tennis shoes.

"Want coffee?" she asked when Jack arrived.

"No, thanks. We have to hurry. I'm double parked."

"Let me finish mine. Otherwise I'm dead."

A pregnant hush hung over the city, broken occasionally by the grinding of a truck in the street, the irregular purrs of automobile motors. People scurried toward the subway kiosks, silent, preoccupied, ignoring the grayness overhead, the intermittent twittering of sparrows.

They checked her bag at the tennis court lockers and trodded silently over the gravel path leading to the reservoir, crunching tiny pebbles beneath their shoes.

"Nearly wore spike heels," said Sylvia, her eyes glistening like the dew on the grass.

Jack smiled weakly. He wondered if he had made a mistake. If she were unable to run or complained; if she fell or twisted an ankle, it might finish their friendship. He did not want anything to go wrong.

"Let's begin at a slow trot," he suggested. "Don't overdo it."

"Think you can make a he-man out of a 98-pound weakling?"

He grinned and relaxed. She had sensed his fears and was trying to put him at ease. Was it intuition, a magical insight that women are credited with but which few really seem to possess? Or coincidence or his imagination? No. She was attuned to him in some mysterious and wonderful way and this was frightening because it must be so fragile.

"Better not talk or we'll be out of breath quickly," he said. "Keep your head high and try to breathe naturally."

Then there was another surprise. She ran well, easily, swiftly. She sped lightly over the path as if she had been running all her life, as if she had been trained. But, of course. She was a natural athlete. He had sensed it when they danced. A natural talent in so many respects.

She ran ahead of him. "Whoa, Bessie," he cried. "We have a long way to go." She matched her pace to his; soon he suggested they walk.

"Walk!" she exclaimed.

"Sure, speedy. I don't mean stroll. Walk briskly with good posture and breathing deeply."

"Of the exhaust fumes?"

"The air's better in the park," he said.

They walked awhile and then resumed trotting. Soon he heard her panting, but she kept going without protest. "We'd better walk again," he said.

She pointed to a 20-story white brick apartment house on Fifth Avenue that overlooked the park. "See the penthouse on top," she said, "with the red awning."

"Hu-huh," he murmured.

"I'm going to have it someday," she said. "It rents for $1,200 a month, has six rooms and a spacious terrace and on a clear day I'm sure you can see across the Hudson into Jersey."

"Steep rent for an apartment," noted Jack.

"For me it would be more than a place to live." Her face glowed with an icy ecstasy. "It's a way of life I imagine for myself, high above the city's noise and dirt and struggle, where people would have to come up to see me."

"You might be disappointed up there," he said. "It might be lonely."

"Sometimes I've got to be alone. Sometimes I can't stand people around me, anyone." The tiny lines above her eyes disappeared. "Besides, you can always get people to visit a penthouse."

"Might be roaches in the kitchen sink," he said.

She laughed. "I doubt it. They could be exterminated anyway. I wouldn't live there forever. The rent is too steep. But I'd like to try it. Must be delightful."

"Why that one? Do you know it?"

"No. Never been there and I don't know who's got it now. I could have found out, but it doesn't matter. It's just a goal I've set for myself."

Jack was still puzzled. "But why that one? There are dozens of penthouses on both sides of the park, and thousands over the city."

"Chance, really. Of course, this one is so wonderfully located, close to midtown and my office, and with Central Park for a garden. And Fifth is still one of the best addresses. But I thought I'd better focus on one penthouse in particular, or else I might never get any. So I decided on that one, and no other."

Jack scratched the back of his neck. "What you really want is the money to afford such a place."

"No. I want that apartment. No hedging. No conditions."

"What if I get it for you?" he asked half-seriously.

"Will you?" she mocked. Their eyes met and they laughed.

"Come on gal, run."

Afterward they breakfasted at a drug store.

"You do this every day?" she asked.

"Four or five times a week, weather permitting. Now it's a habit, as natural as brushing my teeth. Want to try it again?"

"Yes," she said. "It was fun. But frankly, I abhor habits."

Jack felt the jostling in the subway like friendly arms about him and he let himself become part of the sway of the train. His triceps tightened as he swung his arms and stretched his legs along the pavement; it gave him a delicious feeling of well-being. He glanced at the bronze plaque glinting over the I.N. building entranceway: a trench-coated correspondent raced with a document in his outstretched hand, a photographer flashed his bulky camera, and hunched over typewriters, two reporters pounded out the endless news. It looked damn good.

The glass-paneled door twirled under his touch. A colorful poster of a laughing young couple strolling arm-in-arm under a leafy green willow reminded him of Sylvia in the park. He refused to be ruffled by the slogan underneath: "Smoke Satans to be sure."

"How are you Charlie old boy." He lifted the elevator operator from his armpits so that he hung like a puppet.

"Easy now Mr. Stopple, I got work to do," said the gray-haired man breathlessly.

Jack let him down. "Work. Work. Work. That's all everybody thinks about here. You keep taking me up and down, Charlie, always up and down. Today I want to go sideways, take me sideways, Charlie."

He started the elevator up. "One day I'll take you sideways, Mr. Stopple. Don't you worry. This elevator can do things." He patted the control handle.

"Don't forget." Jack hummed "Oh what a Beautiful Morning," breaking into song as he reached his department. He slapped Cowels' back but continued on.

"Stopple, it is not a beautiful morning," said Mr. Adams. "It's cloudy and rain is forecast and I wish you'd stop crooning off key."

Jack beamed. "It's not off key, sir, it's on key. And I'm on time, sir. In fact I'm 30 seconds early. These are my – 20 seconds now – and according to the union contract I have not yet come under management's jurisdiction."

Mr. Adams scowled and Jack walked to his desk. He quit humming but the melody raced through his brain, bursting to be heard.

Cowels stopped typing. "My boy, you seem to have been attacked by the June bug. And in May, too. Very serious. Spring fever is my diagnosis. That charming dark-haired wench is at the bottom of it, I suspect. Or are you allergic to all the budding flowers?"

"No comment S.C. The evidence is damaging but I refuse to incriminate myself. The sun's in the heavens, all's right with the … world." Jack ceased chattering and sat down. Mr. Johns had come in. Cowels resumed typing.

The city editor usually arrived at noon, lunched about 2:30 p.m. and departed shortly after 6 p.m. His unexpectedly early arrival tensed the office.

City News almost ran itself; its routines were long established and the staff experienced in emergencies. But Mr. Johns assumed personal responsibility for everything and he insisted upon being consulted at any hour, in the office or at home, if there was the slightest doubt in making a decision. His assistants were reprimanded for overstepping authority in the most inconsequential matters; consequently they avoided even the appearance of initiative.

In a friendly mood Mr. Johns toured his department, inspecting the equipment and his staff. Invariably he talked baseball with the reporter who hated sports or television programs with someone who stubbornly refused to buy a set. At these infrequent moments he encouraged the men to call him "Jack" But at other times he became visibly upset when not referred to as "Mr. Johns." He had dark, penetrating eyes and black ragged eyebrows and a manner of peering over the rims of his eyeglasses that made a reporter uncomfortable.

Mr. Johns sank into the thick red cushions of his Queen Anne armchair, stretching his arms along the carved wooden supports. His fingers curled around the lion head ends. He closed his eyes and leaned back.

"Jackson," whispered Mr. Adams. The city editor opened his eyes. "There's a three-alarmer on the upper West Side. Lunzer's covering. Think we ought to send McCarthy over from his ground-breaking ceremony to help?"

"Where's my typewriter?" asked Mr. Johns.

"Isn't it … around?" Mr. Adams looked vaguely.

"I don't see it Tom. No, I don't see it at all." Mr. Johns rose swiftly; his sudden activity alerted the staff like an electric shock.

The reporters used an assortment of ancient machines; one took the best he could find when he came to work. But Mr. Johns had a personal typewriter: his award from the Long Island State School of Journalism in 1938 for describing garbage disposal rackets. His name was engraved on its black steel frame in gold letters. On weekends he locked the machine in a cabinet but on weekdays he merely removed the roller and hid it in his desk.

Mr. Johns started around the room, inspecting the typewriters and questioning the reporters. Several stopped their work to aid the search. "That's all right boys," he announced, "continue your work. I'll find it."

After stalking his department, Mr. Johns entered sports. A few minutes later he returned, wheeling the machine on its metal table. "It was just standing there," he told Mr. Adams. "Nobody was using it. It was just standing in a corner, as if somebody purposely concealed it to annoy me."

"Yeah?" Mr. Adams tapped his foot. "Now about this three-alarmer....."

"Who would want to take it?" asked Mr. Johns.

"ahh... the typewriter?" responded Mr. Adams. "I have no idea."

Mr. Johns pressed several keys gently. He unlocked his desk and adjusted the black roller into the machine. Then he shifted the carriage carefully. He inserted a sheet of paper and tested the action. Everything seemed in order. He turned to Henry Twist, the chief copy reader. "Any ideas?"

Twist screwed up his face and rubbed the stubble of his beard. Twist became a reporter following his bankruptcy during the depression at retailing ladies lingerie. Lacking a formal education he apparently had memorized much of his dictionary and a dozen grammars. His talent for anticipating the boss' wishes aided his advancement, but he could never live down his past. Many needled him with questions about college life or women's undergarments and perhaps to retaliate, he became the office tattletale.

"I didn't actually see anybody take the machine," Twist began in his slow whine. "But Stopple was laughing and singing and pretty excited about something this morning. Of course I don't know what it was about ...." He drew out his last words.

"Laughing and singing," muttering Mr. Johns. "I don't understand why anyone should disobey my orders regarding this typewriter." Then he yelled, "Stopple."

Mr. Adams butted in, "Think I ought to send McCarthy on that three-alarmer. I've got him on the phone."

"Hold him," snapped Mr. Johns. The city editor questioned Jack who insisted he knew nothing about the disappearance. He was about to return to his desk when Mr. Johnson asked, "By the way, what were you laughing about earlier today?"

Jack grasped the back of his neck. "I don't remember laughing this morning."

"You don't?"

"No sir."

"Weren't you singing, or agitated about something?"

"Well, I might have been." Jack was about to mention his workout with Sylvia but he paused. It was none of Johns' damn business why he was agitated, or if he was. He stared hard into the boss' eyes. Mr. Johns rose abruptly.

"All right, Jack." He circled Jack's shoulders. "Thanks very much for your help," he added, smiling broadly.

Jack returned to his desk, annoyed, but also relieved that the interview was over. The boss' smile faded quickly and he fretted for some time afterward, holding his head in his hands, suddenly straightening up, pacing behind his desk. Finally, after discarding several attempts, Mr. Johns typed the following notice for the office bulletin board:

"The typewriter belonging to Mr. Jackson Johns, I.N City Editor, is not to be handled by any unauthorized person. His name is engraved on the machine; it is his personal property. It is neither to be moved or removed or used by any unauthorized person. Anyone disobeying these instructions will be subject to severe disciplinary action."

Chapter 9

Two public relations men, one representing the Pennsylvania, New York and Oregon Railroad, the other, the Brotherhood of Freight Loaders, sat before a table reserved for the press. They welcomed Jack with smiles and handshakes and made room between them. Jack was the only reporter at the New York Authority hearing, but he wasn't surprised. The railroad's application to discontinue freight service at three upstate locations did not promise fireworks and his presence protected all newspapers.

Jack was unacquainted with the publicity men but one said he recalled Jack's bylines. The error or lie pained him but Jack didn't contradict the man. Both presented summaries of their client's position. The railroad contended that its freight service was losing money and only duplicated other delivery services. The union said its discontinuance would inconvenience the public and lead to arbitrary dismissals of railroad workers. The last argument, Jack knew, would not influence the Authority. But he was grateful for the releases, which, though partial to one side, saved him the tedious job of determining the issues.

Attorneys for both sides made opening statements and then challenged one another in legal maneuvering that lasted until the hearing examiner ordered a two-hour lunch recess. Both press agents offered to buy Jack's lunch. He replied that it made no difference to him. "Okay," said one, "let's flip." The other agreed and tossed a half dollar into the air. "Heads," called the railroad agent; he won. Jack promised to lunch with the union man at the next hearing.

They dined at a nearby restaurant frequented by business and professional men. The press agent ordered a martini. Jack declined a drink.

"Say, you sure you're a reporter," the press agent said slyly.

"Ha, ha. Only kiddin' ol' man." He told about his years as a reporter in the "old days." "Course, it wasn't so long ago, now that I think of it. Ha, ha. I'm not so old, you know. Ha, ha."

Jack discovered he had only to grunt an occasional "yes" or "un-huh" and the press agent would continue.

"Now you take a dull hearing like this one," he said.

"Crap, n'est-ce pas? Now in my day we'd do one of two things. Either take off for a dame or a bar or a movie and get a fill-in later from the p.r. man. Or, if you were buckin' for a raise, liven the thing up, ya know, put that air of crisis into it. Get some guy to say the whole damn railroad is gonna go broke and thousands of commuters will be left stranded and workers thrown off their jobs. All of these crumbly freight stations get shut. Not so far fetched at that. Scare the public silly, see, then ya got a story. And the editors appreciate it. 'Course it's easier if you're on an international beat. Atomic bombs and stuff. But it works on the home front too, n'est-ce pas? Pardon my French. I worked over there for two years and never could get those frog expressions outta my head... Now don't get me wrong. I'm not tellin' you how to write this thing. Hell, no. I know how mad you guys get at that. Was the same way myself. Hell, no p.r. man would tell me how to work. What's he want for a free lunch? Ha, ha. But that's the way we did it. Great days. And let me tell you, the big boys in the game are still playin' it that way. Crisis, see?

"Everything's a crisis… damn good roast beef, n'est-ce pas? Yesiree. Doomsday is a big seller."

He wiped the gravy off his lips. "Say, now it comes to me. Didn't I see you at the press club ball? No? I coulda sworn I'd seen you there. Great affair. Wouldn't miss it. You goin' this year? Yeah, well you should. Always a good time. I'm sponsoring' two guys on the Express, Barnes and Steeps. They're on the railroad beat, ya know. But don't let me tell you what to do. Ha, ha. Not me. I'm not that sorta guy."

He signed for the check with one of his credit cards. There was another half hour before the hearing was scheduled to resume and the brokerage office of Mahoney and Kahn where Bill worked was only three blocks away. Jack thanked his host for the meal and said he would meet him later.

"Sure, no hurry. I'll fill you in."

Bill's desk was cluttered with newspapers, forms, annual reports, business magazines, so that its green blotter was obliterated. "Hi, have a seat," he said, pointing to a chair with a hand that held a sandwich; his other hand grasped a telephone receiver.

"Yes, I'd buy it," he said over the telephone. "It's acting great in this dull market. With patience it should be good for ten points easy… Well, if you feel that way, buy only fifty shares. We can always buy more on the way up…. Yes, or average down…. Fifty, then…. At the market?…. Right. Call you later…. 'Bye."

Bill scribbled on an order blank and then pushed through the lunchhour throng to a window cage in the rear. Jack watched the ticker tape transactions moving across the front wall screen.

"Market looks lower," noted Jack.

"Yes," replied Bill, pulling his wooden swivel under him.

"Encouraging. Forming a real solid base." Bill was a chartist. He plotted the daily action of the stock market and also the movements of individual securities. From the resulting graphs he forecasted ups and downs. His reference to a "base" indicated that the market was consolidating.

"What do the charts show?" asked Jack.

"Good patterns. Should be hitting strong resistance to the downside soon. If we hold at the 600 level, we'll be ready for a fine upthrust."

"What if it doesn't hold?" asked Jack.

"That would indicate downward action." Both watched the wall tape's changing figures as they conversed. "But it should hold. We have a triple bottom, you know. Much stronger than a double bottom."

"But it could be penetrated," argued Jack. "Then we'd have real trouble."

"True. Then the bottom would be reversed and have the effect of a triple top which would be tough upside resistance" He gulped his coffee. "Want lunch sent in?" Jack said he had eaten. He inquired about his own stocks and Bill got him the latest quotations. Several times they were interrupted by telephone calls; occasionally Bill handled two phone conversations at once, a receiver in each hand.

"Sure the stock is eight points below our price, Mrs. Buscher, but we must have patience…. It's a blue chip company…. I'm certain they're not going out of business…. But how could I possibly know it would decline?…. You have nothing to worry about. Yes, I'm positive of that…. Well, it was 47 at the opening, but now it's 46 5/8…. Yes, that's lower…. Yes, I certainly will watch it…. Carefully, yes…. Goodbye."

Bill slammed the receiver. "God! These customers are driving me nuts!" He leaned toward Jack. "I could make a million bucks in this market. I swear it Jack. I've got the feel of it. If I could only keep my mind on it. But these customers! Christ Almighty! What the hell do they want? I'll tell you, Jack. They want me to make 'em rich. Every last housewife and soda jerk wants me to make 'em rich. And without bother. They have no instinct, no imagination. A stock goes up and they get nervous and want to cash in. A stock goes down and they get scared and blame me. Me! Damn it, Jack, if I had the guts I'd junk this table and telephones and go it alone. I could make it, I tell you. I could. I know it."

A telephone call interrupted him. Jack appreciated his friend's irritability. The smoke and stuffiness, the telephones jangling, the bells, the stock tickers whirring by, the blur of muffled conversations, and finally, the prodding of customers; what an ordeal!

"Don't buy Soyer Drug. Whatever you buy, don't buy Soyer Drug." A gray-haired plump lady seemed to be speaking to Jack although she stared ahead at the stream of symbols on the illuminated screens. "All the drugs act like sputniks but Soyer Drug is a drug."

A reply seemed unnecessary. She clutched several sheets of stock market commentary and continued in a monotone. "But if I sell, it will go up. Then it goes. Always. It always happens to me." She turned in her chair toward Jack. "Ya know, Soyer Drug is just waiting for me to sell. But ya want to know, I'm not selling. I'm not going to be fooled again…. Besides I got a big loss."

Jack tried to think of something comforting to say but he could not. She did not seem to care. "If you really want to buy Soyer Drug, wait until I sell. But if I don't sell, it will always be a drug. Got a cigarette?"

Jack replied that he did not smoke; then she turned her chair away from him, bringing their conversation to a definite conclusion.

"There goes Consolidated Americana," said Bill.

The office stirred as the symbol CA appeared repeatedly on the screen.

CA 22 …CA 5s22 1/8 …CA 1000s22 ¼… CA 5000s 22 ½….

"CA at 22 5/8," a broker called out.

"What's with CA?" asked Jack.

"Can't tell," replied Bill, "but it was due for a ride."

He dialed a telephone.

Jack had profited from his investments but he never owned one of those stocks that rocket upward. He favored conservative, older companies that paid substantial dividends and climbed slowly. Bill had never encouraged him to gamble. "I may lose customers but I don't want to lose a good friend," he had said. Sometimes Jack thought he was foolish in not taking more risks. Imagine plunking down your money on a glamorous name and waking up one day rich. Without working, without planning, without effort. Suddenly rich. It was a crazy idea, but it was being done these days. Somebody had written a book about it, a best seller.

"Hello Mr. Stacy? This is Bill Meyers… Fine, thanks. I'm glad I caught you in. Consolidated Americana is acting very well here. Yes, very strong. There it goes at 22 7/8…. Yes, I knew you'd be glad to hear it…. 23, a big block just went by at 23…. What's that? … Yes I know we paid 25 3/8, but this looks like the big move…. Yes, I certainly will… Goodbye."

"What does CA make, refrigerators and appliances?" asked Jack.

"That was years ago. Don't think they produce anything now. That makes them more valuable. They've got lots of cash, I'm told, and have been losing money for years."

"How can they have money if they've been losing for years?"

"The losses were mostly bookkeeping. They wrote off huge sums when they sold their appliance plants. Now they've got cash and huge losses to write off against future profits. They can make fat profits for five years without paying Uncle Sam a cent in taxes. It's a dynamic situation and the tape indicates a merger or takeover or something in the wind."

"Think I should buy some? asked Jack.

"You can't get hurt. But it's speculative. Right now it's selling at thirty times last year's losses, which is discounting a lot."

Consolidated Americana appeared on the screen tape almost as often as all the other stocks together. But after touching 23 7/8 it slipped fractionally and some volume declined.

"Profit-taking," noted Bill. "You've got a date with Sylvia tomorrow night?"

"Yes. And you're seeing her roommate. Marsha suggested we make it a double."

"I know. Sounds fine." They decided to meet at a midtown Japanese restaurant. "Afterward we can go to my place, added Bill. "I'll take the rug and you can use the .... Damn it... CAs starting to slide."

"You're operating huh?

"I don't know about you pal, but I'm going to make it. Did you know she's divorced?"

"Who?" asked Jack.

"Marsha. Who do you think I'm talking about? That means smooth sailing. Now look at that damn CA.... back at 23 before you can take a breath. What's with Sylvia?"

"She worked out with me yesterday morning at the reservoir."

"What! Got up at dawn? That dame? She is either nuts or in love, boy. Either case you're in the saddle. It's up to you to ride."

Chapter 10

The electric skillet sizzled as the Japanese waiter poured soy sauce and broth over the mixed greens and raw beef. In answer to Marsha's questions, he pointed out the ingredients and cited the recipe. She made notes in a tan leather covered pad.

"I thought you knew all about cooking," said Bill, toying with his second martini.

"I do, silly, but this is foreign."

"Oh," said Bill disdainfully. He gulped the last of his drink.

The aroma of the sukiyaki bubbling in its juices excited their appetites and when it was finally served they devoured it greedily. All except Marsha.

"Did I tell you about the boy reading 'Lady Chatterley' in my class. An unexpurgated version, too. I confiscated it…. Well, I had to. We were doing arithmetic. He looks like you, Jack. The boy. But he's only ten. His hair falls over his forehead like yours. Besides I wanted to read the book…. I'll give it back when I'm finished…. It's better than arithmetic, sure, but it's really pretty silly, when you think about it, the book."

They were sipping tea when Bill suggested they go to his place. "We can dance or watch TV and have some drinks."

"Can we roast marshmallows over the fireplace?" asked Marsha.

"I don't have a fireplace."

"Oh," she said dejectedly. Then she brightened.

"Marshmallows are out of season anyway."

Bill scowled. "Are you for real?" The others laughed.

Marsha's smile brought out a dimple on her cheek.

"Why don't we take in a movie?" suggested Sylvia. "The new mystery at the Rialto got good reviews."

"If that's the picture with lots of Indians it must be marvelous," exclaimed Marsha.

"You're big for Indians, huh?" Bill's index finger tapped his tea cup.

"These are real Indians, from India." Marsha faced Sylvia and Jack opposite. "Do you know the sacred cows of India aren't so sacred anymore. People in India used to get off the sidewalks to let them pass, remember? Well, they keep them off the streets now. I read it only this morning in the New York Mail. That newspaper has more interesting things in little corners. At the end of the dullest stuff about the International Bank or some political meeting is just a sentence maybe, about India or something else just as fascinating. I tell my pupils to search for the hidden treasures in the Mail. Is that the paper you work for?"

Jack explained that he worked for a wire service that supplied news to the Mail and all other newspapers, but did not publish news.

"I guess that's why I never saw your byline," she added.

Jack replied that bylines were subject to the whims of copy readers, editors and policy makers. Local newspapers, including the Mail, often put the bylines of their own reporters on wire service stories to give their readers the impression that their staff is larger or busier than it actually is.

"I know a reporter on the Daily Bulletin who gets his name on every major crime story they print, even if he's on vacation," he added.

"But that's unfair," exclaimed Marsha. Jack shrugged, but Sylvia said many publicity agents write copy for newsmen who take the credit. "It's part of the game," she said.

Bill paid the check, having agreed beforehand to split expenses with Jack. The girls still favored the movie but Bill insisted there would be a long wait outside the theater. Finally, he prevailed. Since neither he nor Jack had taken his car, Bill suggested a taxi.

"It's a fine night," said Jack. "Why don't we walk?"

"It must be three miles from here," exclaimed Bill. "I have very high heels on," added Marsha. But Sylvia said she didn't mind walking "for awhile" and they decided to meet the other couple at the apartment.

As they taxied down Fifth Avenue, Bill slid his arm around Marsha's shoulders and pulled her toward him. They kissed until the cab's sudden halt jarred them apart.

"You sure kiss nice," whispered Bill.

"I know," she replied.

"You don't have to be so conceited about it!"

"I'm not conceited. All my boy friends say I kiss well."

"All your boy friends! How many have you?"

"Only you and another boy now." She smiled. "I meant in the past."

"You never mentioned your past."

"I told you I was married and divorced and all that."

"All what?"

"You can't expect me to tell you everything," she said in a huff. The rest of the way they sat separate and in silence.

Bill thought about "everything."

Comfortable and a bit sluggish, Jack linked hands with Sylvia as they strolled south on Sixth Avenue. They paused at a pet shop window watching dachshund and poodle puppies dash about a straw-covered display pen, smelling and biting each other, crouching in a corner and then springing up, discovering their legs and eyes and noses and mouths and the strange world they had been thrust into. Occasionally a dog stopped to stare out the window, as if frozen, gazing at the humans with that incredulous animal look, full of longing and disbelief; then it would jump back into the reality of the pen.

"They want so little," mused Sylvia. "Just to play and get some attention."

Jack bent and kissed her neck, underneath the dark swirls of her hair. She gripped his hand tighter but continued to watch the animals.

"What do you want" he asked, smiling, as they walked on, "besides a penthouse on Fifth Avenue?"

"The same things most girls want – love, happiness, success." Her eyes glowed in the dusk like polished steel; they searched his. A neon light flashed in their faces.

"I do want to succeed," she said. "I want to do things, all sort of things. I can't even tell you what. I want to be strong. I want to be myself; I want to feel I'm not a leaf buffeted by every silly wind." She turned away, as if suddenly self-conscious. "Does that make sense?" Her voice lilted archly.

"Yes," he said. "You want to prove yourself."

They strolled past several stores, a delicatessen, a bank, a towering office building with a Florentine fountain gushing in front; they walked in the midst of a whirl of humanity, traveling in all directions, singly, in pairs; they heard the grinding of motors, the screeching of brakes, the clip-clop of metal heels on the cement pavement.

"I'm like a mountain climber who seeks summits," she said.

"He doesn't really know why he does it; it's not a particular reward he's after. Only the knowledge he can get up there... I suppose my penthouse is sort of a mountain. I never thought of that. But once I get there I know I'll be bored. I'm sure I'll want to escape, search a new peak. It's always been that way with me."

"What a terrible thing," said Jack, "losing the spark that once fired you. It makes success resemble failure. You begin to doubt – everything…. I always wanted to be a reporter. Even as a kid I lost my delivery route because I read more newspapers than I delivered. I located the newspaper offices in Oakland and hung around the way most boys frequent baseball fields. I would sneak into the buildings and hide, watching the printers set type and the big presses roll. I followed reporters on stories. I was always a reporter on the school newspaper."

His face brightened. "How proud I was as a reporter in the high school play, prouder even than when I won my letter in basketball. It was a bit part, only about four lines, and nobody wanted it. But I rejoiced in it. I battered one of my father's hats for the play. Was he mad! But then I knew all reporters wore a battered hat. Am I boring you?…. Thanks…. Well, to cut it short, I made it, climbed my peak…. Lately though, strangely, my view has faded…. a damn uncomfortable feeling…."

"Perhaps you haven't taken a good look up there," she said. "Maybe you're fogged in and don't realize it. We were talking about bylines at dinner. It's important for you to get them. That's how a reporter builds his reputation. And reputation is everything in this world. Have you thought of developing a specialty, writing features? You're keen on health and exercise. I'm sure you could work up a Sunday piece. We could do it together."

"You may be right," he said. "Perhaps I haven't played all the angles."

"I am right," she said. "I'm also tired Mr. Athlete."

They taxied the rest of the way to Bill's apartment.

Bill's apartment on the tenth floor of a section of a sprawling housing development rented as two-and-a-half rooms; it was actually a parlor adjoining a bedroom-anteroom and a kitchenette. Dominating the Swedish modern furnishings was a huge polar bearskin rug with attached stuffed bear head.

"If you don't behave, he bites." Bill pointed to the white fangs. He had doffed his dark suit jacket for a sporty corduroy. "How 'bout some drinks folks. Don't be bashful. I can fill all desires."

Marsha requested scotch on the rocks. "I'll pass," said Sylvia. Bill looked pained. "Don't be a teetotaler Syl. Jack's very broadminded."

"The usual for me William," said Jack.

"Make mine the same," said Sylvia, laughing.

"Scotches for us and ginger ales for the children." Bill returned from the kitchenette with a tray and a white towel over his arm.

"I don't like scotch," said Marsha.

"But you asked for it," exclaimed Bill. "Didn't she?"

"I know. I just mean I don't like the taste of it."

"Well, why did you ask for it? I told you I've got everything."

"Discipline," she replied. "If I force myself to do things I don't like, when I do things I like I enjoy them so much more."

"That makes sense," said Bill in a tone that indicated the opposite. He set ten records on his automatic phonograph, carefully rolled up his bearskin rug, and took Marsha to dance. Though Jack cha-chaed poorly, Sylvia encouraged him, counting the rhythm aloud to help him keep step.

"You're starting your first cha too late Syl," Said Marsha.

"Dance your own," she retorted.

"But it throws me off honey." She turned her back to Bill and he followed her in step to the music. When she turned again to face him he continued forward as if he had not noticed. They collided in his arms.

"What happened?" Marsha cried. She made no effort to disengage herself.

"Immovable forces," he replied without releasing her. They danced awhile longer and then sat and smoked cigarettes. "Wow," he shouted. "Drinks gone. Papa William fix quick." He brought two more scotches. "More medicine for baby." He placed a tall glass before Marsha. "Children want more bubbly water?"

"Spike mine with rye this time, will you?" asked Sylvia.

"Will I? Now you're talking!" He cupped his hand to his mouth and whispered. "Let's get rid of these two and have ourselves a ball."

Marsha pouted. "Anytime you want to get rid of me, Mr. Meyers, just say the word."

"Ahhhhh, little Marshie's feelings are hurt." Bill gulped his drink and kissed her loudly on the cheek.

Then Bill tuned a horror movie on television, unrolling his bearskin rug for them to sit on. The film appeared to have been produced as a silent: the actors' expressions of love and hatred and fear were so obvious. But dialog had been dubbed in. On the screen, detective Dick Nightingale promised to locate Professor Smithers, whose hobby was transferring human brains into animals. The scientist's daughter, Cynthia, eyelashes flickering, lips trembling, hands pressed to her breast, whispered, "I love you Dick."

"Think she means it?" quipped Jack.

"No," replied Marsha. "Obviously she's under the influence of the monster."

They laughed at the most dramatic scenes and ignored the commercial interruptions until midnight. Then Jack said he "hated to be a killjoy" but he had to work "later on today." Sylvia did not object to leaving but Marsha remained.

When the others had gone Bill refilled their drinks and left the bottle of scotch nearby. He shut the lights so that the television screen provided the only illumination.

"Alone at last," he said, resting his glass on the floor. He circled Marsha's neck and leaned backward so that they tumbled together. She tried to rise but he restrained her.

"Don't you want to see how it comes out?" she asked.

"I know how it comes out." He kissed her, encircling her body.

"I have the feeling I'm not the first girl on this rug," she said.

"The very first," he whispered. She started to utter something but he kissed her again. His hand stroked her hips.

"No, you'd better not come up," said Sylvia.

"You have to get up early, remember? Beside, Marsha and Bill may come soon and…."

He had brushed her neck and now he kissed her ear.

"Nuts to them," he said. She flung her arms about his neck and drew him closer. They kissed a long time.

"Let's go up," he said

"Darling, have patience, huh?" She kissed him hard on the mouth; then she broke away. "No more."

He tried to draw her to him again but she resisted. "No," she said, "no, please no."

He sighed. "You turn off like a lightswitch," he said, a trace of anger in his voice.

"Do I?" Her laughter trickled out. "Do you think so?" She leaned her head against his chest; her hair smelled cool and fresh. "I don't mean to. I don't understand myself sometimes. Everything in me longs for you, do you know that you big thick lug? No, don't kiss me, don't.... Just hold me, yes, hold me strong. Kissing isn't necessary, is it? Are there lovers in the world that never kiss?.... I think you're wrong. They just know; that's enough.... No, don't Jack. I can't. Not now, Jack, please. Do you care for me? Just a little? No, don't answer; you don't have to. It was stupid of me."

He drew her up; her eyes were glistening. "It wasn't stupid," said Jack. "Not at all. I do want to answer. I love you. I love you, Sylvia, do you hear?" It was madness, sheer madness. He had never willingly said those words before; they had to be drawn from him, as if with iron prongs. But she was so strange, so wonderful, and he felt he meant every word. For the first time he meant it; he was soaring insanely; he was dizzy, drunk with joy. He folded her light soft body, pressing her against him, inhaling her spirit into his. He felt they were one.

Chapter 11

Next evening Jack and Bill dined at an Italian restaurant in a sidestreet of west Manhattan. Bill ordered a cocktail and lit a cigarette as they waited for the food. Nearby, a gray cat played with a grape, kicking it with a paw, chasing it under the tables and chairs, arching her back as if the green-yellow berry were alive, pouncing on it, only to provoke it again. Finally it rolled under their table and Bill squashed it. The cat ambled to a corner and licked its paws.

"Cats make me nervous," said Bill. "Always have hated them. Smashed my car once trying to hit one. Say, the double date worked like a charm. Thanks for leaving early."

"Had to anyway," said Jack. "You make out?"

"Great, magnificent, tremendous. 'All the Way,'" He crooned the song title. "Marsha is really a good kid. A trifle idiotic. I almost misjudged her. But she is a good kid."

The waiter set plates of antipasto before them. When he left, Bill asked, "and you?"

"I didn't. I like Sylvia, quite a bit."

"What does that mean? I like Marsha too. Because a guy sleeps with a girl doesn't imply he doesn't like her. That's grammar school psychology."

"I have a feeling about Sylvia – a good feeling. When the right moment comes, she'll come too." Jack smiled. "You go for Marsha, huh?"

"But not your way. Not the pure God Almighty way. Jack, sometimes you're too damn sober for me."

"What the hell has my not drinking to do with it!"

"Relax man. Don't be so literal." Bill sipped his martini. "Take drinking. I'm no souse; you know that. But a shot makes me feel better; eases the pain of sitting all day in that gambling den trying to outsmart the market. People think a broker's a wizard. Wish I was.... All right, so after work I take a few. Drinking to me is like exercise to you; it erases drudgery, simplifies life."

He puffed his cigarette and then crushed it out in the ashtray. "With girls it's essential. You look at a girl and she moves you. She's got shapely legs and you go for legs. Then you speak to her and make progress. Fine. Maybe she likes you – the way your hair's combed or because your shoelaces come untied or some stupid thing like that. That's what girls go for. Then you give her a line and maybe she goes for that. But what next? Listen, I've tried it cold sober and it falls flat. You don't go anywhere. You begin to fence. But she's wary and you're suspicious too. Touché. You strike; she retreats...."

"Gurgle, gurgle."

They laughed. "Right," continued Bill. "It does take the edge off, makes life brighter, the way it should be. Now take last night. If you won't explode I'll tell you something. I made out and you flopped and who's better off and why? You and Sylvia are just as sincere as Marsha and me. But we clicked and you two are still on second base."

"Heading for third," said Jack. "And no hangover."

"Hell, I had no hangover." Bill pounded the table lightly.

"And no regrets, guilty feelings or any of that stuff. On the contrary, I feel great. Life's worth the fuss. Marsha feels the same way. She should, anyway, unless she's been conditioned wrong. No harm's been done. As for the future, you can't be sure you'll be alive tomorrow, so how can you figure out anything else?"

"Live for today for tomorrow we may die. That's one of your hoary sermons, isn't it Reverend?"

"Oh, cut it out." Bill smiled. "Besides there's lots of truth in the hoary sermons, and you know it."

After dinner they saw the mystery film at the Rialto.

Sylvia had promised to run with Jack the following morning, Sunday, but she telephoned him to cancel the date. Important work would take several hours, she explained; they agreed to meet in the afternoon.

Replacing the receiver, she went to her desk and removed a sheaf of papers from her attaché case. The article was finished; it had been trimmed and polished, typed clean and approved by her boss. Now she had to recopy it, in pencil or ink or perhaps on the typewriter, but with errors scattered about, lines crossed out, so that it would appear to be an early draft.

Her assignment had been to integrate the Jeff H. Gyms into a piece on health and exercise tactfully enough to avoid the appearance of publicity. She had toiled for a week on the 800 words and was satisfied. But the crucial task remained – to place it with a wire service. If Intercontinental News distributed it as a Sunday feature, the Jeff H. trademark would be read by millions of prospective customers in hundreds of newspapers with the impact of news and the advertising stigma removed. Coupled with her other work, a batch of newspaper clippings presented to the Hanford executives could result in a bonus or raise. At best she might realize her dream – exclusive control of the account.

From Ann Rawley's casual description of Jack, she thought he could help her. Now that she knew him and liked him there was no doubt. Moreover his help could be as important to his career as to hers. Perhaps it would launch him as a feature writer or a specialist in health. He would be getting a nationwide byline with a minimum of effort and with a subject he could believe in. He was in a rut; he had admitted it himself. Perhaps this story could make the I.N. top brass take notice of him. But with all her arguments, Sylvia feared that he might misinterpret her motives. True, originally, her plan had been a selfish one. But now it was a joint venture; she was convinced of that. Still she hesitated. He might be too proud to take credit for her work. To prepare for this possibility she planned this subterfuge. The ends justify the means; he had as much advocated it.

Jack was waiting at 86th street and Central Park West when she arrived a little breathless, carrying a folder with her handbag. They kissed swiftly and strolled into the park.

"Finish your work?" he asked.

"Not yet. In fact it's the start of a project. I brought it along. Perhaps you would look at it?"

"Sure. Be glad to help."

"You can. It's on exercise as a means to better health and I'm angling it for a newspaper."

He grinned. "In that case I'm an expert."

"You are. Though you seem to joke about it. Not everybody could be a reporter for Intercontinental News. And you certainly know plenty about exercise. You should be proud."

He slipped his arm around her waist and drew her against him as they walked. "I am proud – of you. My father always said I needed a press agent."

"You do." She smiled and looked up at his handsome face; his chiseled chin gave him that strong, determined appearance, she decided, and the deep cleft emphasized it.

"I dislike them," he said, "present company excluded of course."

"What's wrong with press agents?"

"Too human. They always want you to do something for them."

Sylvia changed the subject. It was a sunny spring day, an ideal walking day, and the park was bustling with youngsters and their parents, couples wheeling baby carriages, walking arm-in-arm; old men sitting on the wooden benches, smoking and reading newspapers. They passed a huge grassy circle where several baseball games were in progress and continued eastward, stopping finally at the edge of a playground.

"Ever watch children playing?" he asked. "Not that I'm queer you understand, but I can watch them for hours."

"Your maternal instinct coming on. Don't know why but kids depress me."

They sat beside a young woman engrossed in the picture story of the fourth happy marriage of movie star Lana Swanlor. Her child, three or four years old, molded sandpiles at her feet. He would fill a tiny red pail from the sandbox in the middle of the playground, lug it to the bench and overturn it, though never quickly enough to make a neat pile. He seemed to get a tremendous satisfaction in flipping the pail, despite his lack of success. Invariably after dumping the sand he clasped his hands silently and ran for more.

"Want to see my copy?" asked Sylvia. Jack said yes and she withdrew the sheets from the folder. His lips moved slightly as he read.

When he had finished he said, "not bad."

"Do you think it overplays the company aspect?"

"On the contrary," he replied. "If I were Jeff Hanford I'd expect more of a plug in my ad."

Two lines deepened in her brow. "This isn't an ad. I thought it would make a news feature."

"It could," said Jack.

The little boy tossed his pail next to Jack's foot and Jack leaned forward and rubbed his short-clipped red hair. The child looked up and smiled, displaying several unevenly spaced teeth; then he grabbed his pail and ran for the sandbox.

"Does it need changing?" asked Sylvia.

"No. Fine as is. 'Course an editor would alter it here and there. They all do. Should be perfect for the woman's page."

The woman's page! The last place she wanted. She felt the sun warming her uncomfortably. "Could this be a Sunday feature – for a wire service?"

"Sure," he replied, stretching his arms above his head and his legs out stiffly and yawning.

"Jack, if you don't like the story, why don't you say so? You don't have to be polite."

"I'm not being polite Syl. Copy's fine. Gee, it's warm today.... Maybe I'm not the best judge, though, I've never written publicity."

"But this isn't publicity," she insisted. "It's news, or rather, a feature. What if you had written it for I.N.?"

"That's different. For one thing, you mention the Jeff H. Gyms as if they were the only places to exercise in the whole country. That's good public relations I suppose, but it wouldn't do for a wire service story."

"Now we're getting somewhere," she said. "How would you change it?"

"Bring in the Y's, the athletic clubs, the facilities at schools and colleges, even the parks and playgrounds."

"But the Jeff H. Gyms could be included in an I.N. feature?"

"Yes." He paused. "Though other commercial gyms might holla if only one were named."

"It wouldn't please the client if we mentioned others," she thought aloud. "What about the rest of it? For I.N.?"

"Fine. Oh, maybe a few minor changes."

"Then why don't you use it?"

"Me?" He laughed softly. "But this is your baby."

"But you've got the same ideas about the importance of exercise, right? Beside, you can change it, restyle it; it's only a first draft.

"You'd want the Jeff H. Gyms left in, wouldn't you?" he asked, a slow smile spreading over his face.

"You said it would be appropriate." She hesitated, then she added as offhanded as she could, "if you're convinced it shouldn't be there, well take it out."

"But I don't' get paid to write features."

"And you don't get bylines. And outside of your boss and a few friends, nobody knows you. How are you going to build a reputation? How are you going to get ahead in the news business?"

"I don't know if I want to get ahead. Where is 'ahead' anyway? Becoming a desk man or assistant editor or a minor executive juggling somebody else's copy all day, shuffling men around like a deck of cards, concerned with increasing income or answering the dull correspondence of out-of-town editors and publishers? I like reporting well enough; at least there's a variety of assignments. As for features, I don't know if I'm slick enough."

"But you never will know unless you try," she cried.

Suddenly she saw his face like a comic mask. Under the flushed cheeks and smooth skin and sturdy jaw was a terrible flab. Of course! Like the other he-men she had known, he was a phony. Frightened and weak, trembling at the idea of something new. But then she discovered that she was not repelled. She wanted to succeed with the Jeff H. account, but she wanted Jack Stopple too. Had she sensed the frailty beneath his physical strength from the beginning? Had she been aware of the essential weakness of the others, too, and instead of being disgusted had she been stimulated? What she had to face now was the possibility that Jack would flatly refuse the Jeff H. story. Of course he was not the only I.N. reporter. The grapevine said that one horseplayer was constantly in debt and that another could be approached via the bedroom. She hoped to avoid the shopworn contacts. Still, they were available if all else failed.

She could play it straight, submitting the story through the regular channels, buying a few lunches and plugging away by mail and telephone. But that was rarely effective these days; there were just too many publicists and the news outlets were diminishing. She could try another wire service and if that failed, a local newspaper. It would still be publicity, though not the splash she wanted. She knew she had to anticipate setbacks, but still she believed she had not erred with Jack. They were both climbing and they could boost each other. But perhaps she had overstressed the logic of the situation. In trying to make it clear to him she might destroy the affection between them. They had passed beyond a business relationship and she would be mad to argue on that basis. Clearly she had to change tactics; she had to pass the initiative to him.

"Let's not argue," he said. "I'll think about it."

She smiled and rested her head on his shoulder. "You're the boss," she said.

At that moment the boy overturned his pail on Jack's foot and the sand trickled into his shoe. The boy looked up, fright in his eyes. But Jack's surprise became a smile; he untied his shoelaces and shook out the sand.

"G'wan and play," he told the boy. "I deserve that."

Chapter 12

As they strolled southward along the outskirts of the park Jack considered the disquieting possibility that Sylvia's sole interest in him might be to publicize the Jeff H. Gyms. He was hardly the most qualified reporter she could reach, nor the most influential. But, as she had pointed out, neither was his position inconsequential. She was ambitious, admittedly so, but she was also frank. She had disclosed her publicity job from the beginning and had requested his aid. But now that he thought of it, they had never discussed the intricacies of exercise and his assistance to her in the field had been in the most general of terms. What then was the quality of aid she wanted?

In its present form, her article was vague about exercise and still vaguer about its benefits to health. But it was quite clear about the Jeff H. Gyms. Of course he could rewrite the piece, fusing his ideas and knowledge of the subject into her generalities and salesmanship. But the result would be a more polished plug. Though she had denied it, he knew that if he dropped the commercial angle she would be terribly disappointed.

He had never written an I.N. feature; it was not expected of him. His job was spot news, the fast breaking story; there were specialists who handled features. But if he submitted one, well written, he did not doubt that it would be used. He would gain nothing tangible but the deed could conceivably help his career. He would be getting a byline, his first I.N. byline, for all features were signed. It would be a chance for his parents to see his name in an Oakland newspaper; that, perhaps, would make the effort worthwhile.

There was little risk involved; even if he included the Jeff H. plug, he could do it unobtrusively. Exercise was a logical subject for him to write about; several staffers knew about his athletic endeavors. No one would suspect an ulterior motive.

Still, he wished he could erase the taint of commerce from his relations with Sylvia. It was as a woman that she attracted him and he hoped that it was as a man that she wanted him. He had felt her respond to his kisses. Could she love him as he was? She was enthusiastic about her work and she was climbing toward some mythical penthouse success. But she did not consider it a myth. In the world of publicity, illusion was peddled as truth and if the product sold, that truth was indistinguishable from illusion. She wanted him to share her folklore, to be a success. But her idea of success, at least in the field of reporting, was outdated. The pioneer days of journalism were over; it was strictly business now. The era of the carousing reporter who lived in bars and brothels and became a celebrity overnight with a sensational story was gone. This was the age of job security, the guaranteed annual wage, the pension plan. The union negotiated wage increases, regardless of the work he did. And what, finally, was the difference between $100 a week or $150 or $200 with a system of graduated taxation?

I am today's reporter, he wanted to shout to her, more efficient than the old model though less glamorous. I must come to work on time and perform without hysterics. I'm on the production line and I produce the news like a good mechanic makes trucks. Success in my field is spored over cocktails and codified by contract; reputations are promoted by publicity and hoax. What did an occasional feature or byline matter?

They had not spoken for some time. Now Jack took Sylvia's hand, a casual gesture, as they fell into step. Before them a youngster in pigtails struggled on stilts. Wary of the pavement's indentations, the girl stepped haltingly forward: one, two, three movements, then she stopped and smiled broadly. A trickle of sweat wetted her cheek. She rested high on the wooden boards as Sylvia and Jack passed.

"I guess I'm not your idea of a knight in shining armor," he said. "Perhaps you could think of me as a modern hero – wrapped in aluminum foil."

She laughed. "Everybody wants happiness," he continued, snipping a twig off a bush. "But nobody is sure what it consists of or where to find it."

Her smile seemed forced. "You sound as if you had the secret."

"Sometimes I think I'm close to it. Sometimes... running around the reservoir, the wind against my face, brisk, the sun invigorating my senses. I feel so alive and good and I think, this is it. I've got it; it's really so simple. Now if I can only keep going, like this, on and on, without a plan or a purpose, fast and strong for the rest of my life, I'll be happy, supremely happy."

"Then you get winded," she said. They laughed.

"How did you guess? It's silly but so true. My breath comes short and hard, my legs begin to ache, the pounding of my heart becomes unbearable and the sun is suddenly a fiery enemy. I want to keep going; I try and try. But I can't. My happiness is over."

"You shower and cool off and subway to the office."

"Yes, of course. That's how it is; that's how it always is." He swept her in his arms, suddenly, there on the path with boys and girls skating around them, gawking at the strange adult behavior: and on the wooden benches people peered around the corners of their magazines and pocket books. He kissed her on the mouth, hard, and she was limp; it was a moment frozen eternally under the maples and oaks and elms bursting with green; then it too was over and they walked on, in step, their arms swinging loosely, near thick flowering bushes atwitter with sparrows, past a proud hopping robin and children jumping into chalk drawn boxes, and others throwing a ball and others skipping rope and a busy tailed squirrel sitting on his haunches observing all in hungry wonder. On a hill, boys explored the rock crevices, searching for the mystery of the search, and others, unmindful of their laundered clothes, flung themselves upon the brown soft earth covered with a new green fuzz and rolled downhill, rolling over and over themselves upon the crisp blades of grass, rolling over and over as if there were nothing else to do, nothing else worth doing, in the whole world.

They came to the bronze statue of Alice in Wonderland and the Mad Hatter, Pausing to watch the children crawl about and under and into the honeycomb. They continued around the sailboat pond, blinded for an instant by the sun's reflection in the shimmering water. Leaning over the side, using rubber tipped poles or their bare arms, young boys pushed their ships toward the sharpies and lone masted skiffs and schooners and huge many-sailed models. They passed a small crowd around a man who electronically controlled a gleaming white yacht; his speedy craft maneuvered between the wind tossed ships and always returned to its owner. Nearby a boy with a yellow shirt and short pants threw a leaf into the pond and yelled to his companions, "look at my sailboat."

They climbed uphill to 72nd street and continued south, passing several playgrounds surrounded by tall black iron fences, under two stone bridges until they reached the zoo. A piercing cry, like that of animal pain, was only an automatic balloon blower, a rocket shaped metallic device that compressed air into the red and yellow and orange spheres, inflating them in a flash.

To the right a low red brick building partly covered with clinging green vines housed a section of wild animals. In one of the narrow outside cages, a Siamese tiger paced back and forth on white-tipped paws, its supple orange-brown body turning the corners with the smoothness of years of practice.

"Beautiful, isn't he?" mused Jack. "His ragged black stripes are like wounds. Look how he carries his head high. I wonder how he feels rubbing against those bars. They hold him prisoner, yet he shows them a kind of affection."

"The cage protects him as well as us," said Sylvia, "against what we would do to him if he were free."

"Yes, it's a home, isn't it, a cage. Can he be at peace there? No, not with peanuts and popcorn flung at his face. Look at his nose, rather delicate, isn't it?" The red lined nostrils seemed to flare. "He was born to be a champion of his race. What a comedown!"

"Not really." said Sylvia. "He looks to me like an overgrown cat. If the keeper slipped the latch one day and he could escape he'd probably be more frightened than the spectators. He'd take a quick look around and decide the safest place was back in the cage."

The tiger flicked his long tail and for an instant his red tongue played over his upper lip and the long white fangs usually hidden in his mouth flashed in the sunlight: then he resumed pacing.

"I'm sure he resented your remark," said Jack.

They strolled to the center of the zoo where two seals swam in a circular pool. A third sat on an elevated cement platform at the edge of the water sunning himself, his small head tilted upward, his nose high in the air as if he were balancing an invisible ball. The swimming seals submerged for a minute or two and then leaped out, honking at the spectators for food. Whether it was thrown or not they immediately flopped back into the water, only to appear later at another spot. Beside Sylvia stood a little blonde girl in a white dress with blue polka dots; a string was knotted around her wrist and a red balloon floated above her. Delicately, as if they were jewels, the girl removed morsels of popcorn from a bag and flung them one by one into the pool, unmindful of the location of the seals.

"Sylvia," said Jack suddenly. "I know it's crazy, but let's go to my apartment."

"It's so lovely out."

"I know. Don't make me explain."

"All right," she said softly.

They left the park quickly. Jacked hailed a taxi on Fifth Avenue and soon they were climbing upstairs. Sylvia stopped at the third floor. "Whew, you are high up," she said.

"I'm not in condition after all."

"I'm sorry," he replied.

For the first time he hated the old brownstone, the creaking stairway and dark narrow hallway and his flat on the top floor. He saw it now as a shabby place, and he wondered why he had not been aware of this earlier. Perhaps he had anticipated the difficulty of finding new and better quarters in this overcrowded city

They reached the door but his key jammed in the lock. A damned conspiracy to rob the joy of his life; he hoped she would not become depressed. He wanted this to be right. Finally the lock clicked open.

"The bed..." He groaned; it was unmade. He threw the blanket up to the pillow and tossed on the faded green bedspread. "Landlady usually makes it ... there... all set."

"For what?" she asked. Her eyes smiled but her face was rather solemn.

"Presentable. That's what I meant."

"Usually presentable when you invite girls up here?"

"Oh don't say that, please don't." He kissed her gently, his lips brushing the corner of her mouth. "Let's not hurt each other," he whispered. "Sit down, sit down." He pointed in the direction of the bed but she sat in the easy chair. "Do you want a drink?"

"No," she replied.

"I may take one," he said, going to the cabinet.

"Don't." The word was a command; she added more softly, "You don't have to."

He knelt beside the wide wooden arm of her chair. "I want you Sylvia. You know I want you."

The silence was punctuated by the ticking of the alarm clock. Her hazel eyes clouded and he thought she was going to cry. But suddenly she smiled, broadly, and then she laughed a little. "I'm here, you see."

Dim streetlights filtered into the otherwise dark room. Except for Jack's argyle socks, they lay naked under the thin bedspread; their clothes, strewn on the armchair and floor, resembled a battlefield. But it had not been a battle, no God no. Jack had slept; he still felt so relaxed he feared he might sink off again into a heavy oblivion. But now he wanted to stay awake; he forced himself to think. So good. Without a word and yet with such unspoken meaning. He felt potent and confident and happy he was a man. He was proud, but not of accomplishing, simply of being. In the midst of their passion he had reaffirmed himself in a mystical communion with the God of creation.

But Sylvia had not been there. He had raced to his destiny alone. But why alone? He wanted her with him, then. He had cried out his love for her, but he had not been conscious of her. Had he lied? He had avowed his love for other girls at that instant of triumph. He had not loved the others; they had been instruments for his communion, essential links perhaps, but only that.

But that was wrong! He wanted to love Sylvia, not to use her. Sylvia had given herself freely, cleanly, so like a human sacrifice and he was so grateful. There must be no sham between them.

He pressed his limbs against hers and kissed her face and neck and shoulders.

She touched him softly. We'd better get up," she said.

"Yes."

They retrieved their garments like torn ticket stubs after a play. Oh God, no, it hasn't been that, and now the curtain's falling. No; it would not be a sad little ending; it was a beginning. The curtain had fallen on the pettiness and self-seeking; it was being flung up, up now, on a new brightness.

Chapter 13

For reason unaccountable to Bill, Marsha was playing hard-to-get. Several times since the night they snuggled in the thick fuzz of his rug she had refused to return to his apartment and once, in response to an outright demand, she had declared that she did not want to sleep with him again. That was woman talk, he knew, chatter to be tolerated but then completely ignored. Nevertheless her behavior was disconcerting and, at the strangest times, while taking an order for 100 shares of XYZ Corp., for example, he would discover himself wondering why their affair did not proceed smoothly once the ice had been broken.

Operating on his pet theory, Bill took her to a waterfront tavern, where surrounded by an assortment of muscular and queerly dressed characters, they downed four or five whiskies. The happy glow of drunkenness descending upon him, Bill suggested the cozier atmosphere of his flat. Instead she challenged him to a game of checkers. His prompt refusal apparently encouraged an eavesdropper to butt in and accept and he had been forced to witness her win two of three matches while a crowd kibitzed.

In despair, Bill decided upon a ruse. He invited her to a party; no girl refused to attend a party. This one, he had explained, was being given by a friend who lived on another floor of his apartment house. Actually, no such affair was scheduled; instead, his friend allowed Bill to tape a note to his door that read: "Mother ill. Party off. Sorry." But with Marsha already in the building, it would be simple to then invite her to his apartment. From there, he was on his own.

Bill removed his gray felt hat in the elevator as they ascended to the fifth floor. He brushed back his crew cut hair and, with somewhat forced gaiety, warned Marsha that his friend was very handsome but that he would be watching them both to make sure that nothing transpired. Secretly, of course, he gleefully anticipated the success of his scheme and began to plan his moves once they reached his own flat. He had employed this ruse twice before and it had worked without a flaw; he did not believe he would have had to resort to this method with Marsha, but he consoled himself with the truism that women were unpredictable and it was this very quality that made them so attractive to men.

The elevator door slid back automatically and as they walked down the well-lit hallway Bill could see the note taped on the door ahead. He slowed purposely to enable Marsha to reach it first.

"5E, apartment 5E, down this way," he said.

When they arrived he added, "will you press the buzzer, dear?"

"There's a note," she reported. But not bothering to read it, she thumbed the doorbell.

Bill shut his eyes as he listened to the chime trip over two notes. He silently prayed that his friend was out. Of course he knew about the scheme and would play along, but still it would be awkward if the door opened. Bill thought desperately of what to say if his friend opened.

Marsha smiled and tried the doorbell again. "Why doesn't she read the note?" Bill demanded silently. The strategy called for her to read it first. He forced a return smile and remarked coyly, "wonder what the sign says?"

"It says, 'party here, ring the bell hard'," she replied.

"It does?" His voice had cracked and he felt the blood draining from his head. He could contain himself no longer.... It was his note, the same message he had planted there hours ago.

"The note says, 'Mother ill. Party off. Sorry'," he observed.

"What made you say the other thing?"

She pulled black-rimmed eyeglasses from her handbag and cleaned them with a slip of chemically treated paper. "Party notes always say something like that." She examined the message.

"Guess the party's off," she added.

"Yes. Too bad."

"Hope she's all right."

"Who?"

"His mother, silly. We should call, I suppose. Know where she lives?"

"No, no. No idea at all."

"Maybe we could look her up in the phone book."

"She lives in Chicago, or Florida. Yes, Miami, Florida. Someplace like that."

"Oh."

"Nothing we can do, absolutely. But, well, let's see now, as long as we're in my house I supposed we might just as well toddle up to ...."

"I know a party," she interrupted.

"Yes, well, since we're here and my place is just a few floors above, we might go there."

"This party is nearby, in the village. Now where is the address?" She began exploring her huge rectangular pocketbook.

"My other boy friend is there."

"Wait a minute. If you think I'm going to a party to compete with your other playmate, stop right there."

"Why? Are you scared? Here, hold these." She handed him a lipstick, an eye glass case and a pocket book entitled, "White Slave Success."

"Interesting literature." Bill encouraged the sneer in his voice.

"Not mine. I borrowed it from that boy in my class; remember? The one who was reading 'Lady Chatterley'? He's very bright. Too bad he's only ten."

She delved deeper into the handbag. "Please hold these too." She gave him a plastic rainhat, a small flashlight and a pink sponge. "I'm sure I put it …in … Here it is!"

Between the tips of her fingers she held a torn envelope as if it were a sparkling gem. "47 Kelly street, apartment 5E. That's the same apartment as this!"

What a coincidence," said Bill. His face was the mask of tragedy. "But we're not going there."

"Where else can we go? I know. There's a new western at the Odeon. Lots of cowboys and Indians. I go for Indians."

"I know."

"They relax me," she added.

"Listen. Let's go to my place while we're deciding. I'll fix a couple of drinks and …."

"What's to decide? If you don't like the movie idea, we could go to a night club. But that would cost plenty and we have this party that's free."

"Money's not involved."

"What then?" A railroad track appeared in her brow; then, as quickly, vanished. "You don't want to meet your rival. There's nothing to be afraid of."

"I'm not afraid of anybody," he insisted. "I suppose he's civilized."

"He's very nice, like you. Good. It's even close enough to walk."

He had a premonition of ill tidings ahead. This was the first time his ruse had failed. Perhaps it was an omen.

They climbed four dimly-lit flights to the top of the brownstone, Bill muttering all the time. "I smell rats lurking in the corners," he said. But Marsha's cheerfulness increased as they got closer.

"Look," she exclaimed. "Now there's proper sign." A huge white poster on the door in block letters read: YES.

"Yes what?"

"It's affirmative, silly. It's philosophically positive."

"I'm sure," said Bill flatly.

The door was ajar and nobody greeted them when they entered. Five high-ceiling rooms ran off the long hallway and in each was a bed or couch, plain wooden chairs and a dresser, as if several occupants shared the flat. Jeans, slacks and open-necked sport shirts seemed de rigueur for both sexes and Bill decided he must be the only male there who had recently shaved. The incongruity of heavy beards and thick mustaches on so many young men's faces lent the party a masquerade atmosphere. In one room a guitarist on a stool strummed "Green Sleeves" while his hushed listeners sprawled on a double bed in various positions of discomfort. In the next room: an intent girl with thick eyebrows waved her cigarette holder like a paint brush. "Were Sartre and Sagan existentialists or communists or what?" she demanded querulously.

"They're intellectuals, isn't that enough?" replied a black bearded young man with obvious disgust.

"I'm sure Camus planned his death," commented a girl in black slacks and shirt and close-cropped hair. "It was so wonderfully absurd."

Bill and Marsha continued down the hallway to a room with an improvised bar. A half-filled punch bowl with a greenish concoction was encircled by several partly consumed wine bottles. A slab of ice with a pick rested on the floor.

"Hi kids. Looks like Park Avenue has come downtown." Ann Rawley, in blue jeans, and a gray sweater, put her arms around both of them.

"Hi," said Marsha.

"I've come to meet my beatnik rival," explained Bill.

"We're going to have it out with broken wine bottles while the chorus chants blank verse."

"Sounds great," said Ann. "What's he talking about?"

"He talking about Andre Blaine," noted Marsha. "I never said he was a beatnik."

"Andre Blaine," exclaimed Bill. "Does he wear a red goatee or a blue one?"

"He's not at all like that. Andre is very sweet."

"Oh. A thweetie. Thay now," he lisped.

"Don't be nasty." snapped Marsha.

"Honey, I hope you're prepared to drink this ghoulish stuff because I intend to finish the only decent liquid on the table." Bill poured the remains of a bourbon bottle into a glass and chipped a piece of ice. Marsha accepted a half glass of sauterne.

"Funny, you together," said Ann. "Does your roommate see Jack Stopple?"

"Yes. They're still going around."

"Makes me a matchmaker, practically." Ann said it without joy but Marsha appeared enthusiastic. "Yes, it does," she said. Bill groaned. "Women," he said, "forever scheming."

Stanley Cowels appeared suddenly, his hair slightly mussed.

"Here you are my western rosebud, my lily of the silver lode. Missed me, didn't you? But I've been faithful; you must believe that, even if it's a lie."

He turned to Marsha, his expression as serious as before; only the brightness in the blue of his eyes betrayed his humor. "Ah, it's you, my favorite school marm. Why didn't my instructors look like you? A pity. How are you? Marsha Golden, isn't it?"

"Yes. Hardly anybody remembers names anymore. How sweet of you Mr. Cowels."

"Stanley or Stan or Boopsie or any dear name that comes to your pretty head. But don't call me mister. I kiss your hand… I'm not so ancient, really. Dye my hair, for effect, don't I sweet Ann?"

"Do you? No, that's real, isn't it?"

"Real?" His eyes opened wide. "My dear Ann, nothing is real, absolutely. It may be optical, apparent, seeming, possible, simulated, but real? No no no, of course not. It's a wig, actually, look!" He lifted his hands as if to remove a hairpiece.

"No, don't," Ann screeched and then suddenly laughed.

"You see, it is real."

They drifted into another room where an artist rapidly sketched a tall thin girl whose dark hair cascaded down her back; they joined a group observing the process.

"There's Andre," cried Marsha. Everyone, even the artist, turned as a young man of medium height, rather stout and almost bald, entered the room. He wore a dark suit with a vest from which a gold chain dangled, a white-on-white shirt and a deep blue tie. His roundish face paled at the sudden attention.

"Hello," he said, swallowing. "Didn't think you'd be here."

"But I am." Marsha's eyes sparkled; her face seemed aglow.

"Andre, I want you to meet William Meyers. You have lots in common." They shook hands stiffly; then she introduced Cowels, who, almost immediately afterward, left the room. Marsha said, "Bill, why don't you show Andre the bar?" When the young men had gone, the girls settled on a couch. Marsha took a cigarette from her handbag and gave one to Ann.

"It's terribly daring of you to mix your boy friends," said Ann. "But isn't it dangerous?"

"Why?"

"What if they fight?"

"Fight!" Marsha choked on a puff of smoke as she exploded in laughter. "About what?" Me? Oh, that's too much!"

"What's so funny?"

"It's hilarious." Her breast heaved as the laughter subsided. "Men don't fight over women. Not in New York. I don't think they do anywhere anymore. Do they still in Nevada?"

"Well…gee, I don't know. I just suppose they did."

"In the movies, honey, in the westerns. That's one reason I like cowboy pictures so much. Oh, the way they do fight over us sometimes, breaking chairs and tables, even killing each other." She giggled. "But not in New York, dear; has it happened to you?"

Ann looked up at the plaster peeling off the ceiling.

"I'm not as popular as you." She brushed her hair away from her eyes. "But if they don't fight they could become friendly and compare notes. You could lose both."

"It's possible," replied Marsha. "But don't be gloomy. New York is a big city; there are so many young men." She inhaled and slowly blew the smoke out her thin nostrils. "I must confess, though, it's an experiment, a spur of the moment decision. I've never done it before. But then, why not? If a scientist never mixed his chemicals he'd never discover anything."

They sipped their drinks silently. "I know it's presumptuous of me," began Ann, "but who do you prefer?"

"That's another thing," she said intently. "I really don't know. Honestly. That's why I thought it would be good for me to see them together. When I'm with one I like him and when I'm with the other I forget about the first. And the strangest thing is that when I'm alone I don't wish for either of them. In fact...," Marsha lowered her voice, "...promise you won't breathe a word...."

Ann shook her head.

"... When I'm alone I can't even remember what they look like. They just seem to vanish, as if they never really existed. It's positively eerie... So bringing them together may have very positive results, don't you think?"

Ann nodded solemnly.

"Stanley Cowels seems an interesting man," said Marsha in an expectant tone, as if to say, I've disclosed some of my secrets and I expect you to reciprocate. When she did not reply, Marsha added, "is he really chasing you or is it my imagination?"

"He is, I suppose," said Ann.

"Well, why so glum. He appears more exciting than most men. Is he a poet?"

"He's a newsman, a good one I think. In my office. I believe he does like me."

"So...."

"Well, he's nice I suppose, underneath. But he's too old for me and he's divorced and has children."

Marsha pondered her remarks. "Age is relative," she said finally. "It's a matter of taste. I have a girl friend who wouldn't go out with a man unless he's at least ten years older. And you shouldn't hold divorce against him. I'm divorced you know. Nearly everybody gets divorced nowadays."

"Funny," mused Ann, a faraway look in her eyes. "My father let me leave Reno because all the men I seemed to meet were divorced. So here I am in New York being chased by another one." She laughed grimly.

"You can't escape your fate. I never worry about such things. Whatever will be will be; twist and turn, you can't escape your fate."

"Just give in?"

Marsha patted her cheek. "No, silly. Be yourself and do what you can, whatever you think is best. But I believe life takes a hand and leads you, eventually.... Take my first husband. He's a lawyer, not a bad one I'm told. Well, he wanted me but I really didn't care too much for him. I liked him and all that, but it was nothing special, you know."

Marsha crushed her cigarette under her heel. "But he was determined. He kept after me and after me and he made all kinds of threats and promises, so finally I had to say yes. I was right, though. I told him I didn't think it would work out and it didn't. But the funniest thing was that he wanted out. He discovered another girl, a new secretary I believe, and maybe she becomes the big flame that I once was. Anyway, he quit me. And after all his promises. So it just shows you never know about things. You can't be too smart."

"Don't take offense, Marsha. I guess I'm old fashioned. But I don't want to be divorced. I want an ordinary life with one man and one family and one house."

"Sure. I'm with you kid. But if it doesn't work out that way, well, no use fighting city hall. Maybe it's your fate to have just that and maybe mine is to have five husbands. There's no telling in advance. But maybe that's the best part of life. I think it would get me down, if I knew what would happen before it did."

"It does get me down, sometimes. Life I mean."

Marsha gave her a little hug. "Maybe you're trying too hard. Don't push it. Ever heard of Zen? It's an oriental religion. I don't go much for religion but I went with a guy once who studied Zen and he said it was foolish to think too much about yourself. In a hundred years it won't matter anyway so why should it matter now? If you put things that way, get that hundred years long view of things, life becomes simpler. Look into Zen. It's a real gloom chaser. There are books on the subject but let me warn you it's tough going. I never finished one but I get ideas from them. Like, all life is a river and it keeps flowing along and we are a part of it. It doesn't pay to buck the tide, see, just flow along and do the best you can. Get the idea?"

Bill led the way into the next room. "Are you French, Andre?" he said, thinking he would be rather patronizing.

"No," he replied with what seemed a pained smile. "My mother insisted on that name for me. She spent her junior college year in Paris and it so twisted her that she forced all kinds of frills on my solid Boston-bred father. He declares she had a lover by that name, but she has always denied it."

Bill nodded. "Amazing how we Americans can be so level headed about our own culture, but throw us a French accent and we suddenly shrink into our inferiority complexes." His commiseration, he thought, had been apt and magnanimous.

"The boys in the office call me Andy. I encourage it. Brings me closer to people, don't you think so?"

"I suppose it does. Where do you work?"

"Walters, Pierson, Neuberg and Mcgee. I'm a customer's man."

"Well, well, well. Small world. I'm with Mahoney and Kahn. Same job."

"That's so. How do you like working for a small house?"

"We're not so small," protested Bill. "We're in six cities now, expanding all the time."

"That so?"

"You bet."

The wine bottles were mostly empty now at the table-bar; even the greenish punch had been consumed. "Not exactly the Ritz," noted Bill. Andre pulled his sleeve. "I've brought my own," he whispered, pulling out a flask. "Not much but it's good. Care to try?"

"Andre, you've just whispered the kindest words I can imagine. I almost forgive you being my rival." They toasted each other's health.

"Known Marsha long?" asked Bill, licking a drop of the liquor off his upper lip.

"Might say that. You?"

"Reasonably so. Nice girl. Very nice."

"I think so." Andre emphasized the "I" so that Bill raised his eyebrows. They gulped their drinks.

"Very sweet," said Bill.

"The whisky?"

"No, Marsha."

"Oh, yes. Very."

Both took another swig. Bill cleared his throat.

Andre glanced around the room. Finally, he said, "What do you think of the market?"

"Hard to say. At the moment, fluctuating." He laughed nervously. "Buyers and sellers. Ha, ha." Andre did not join him. "What are you recommending these days?" asked Bill.

"Not much. Bit cautious these days."

"Yes."

"What looks good to you?"

Bill hesitated. "Gas," he said. "Yes, sir. Big expansion there. Natural gas, a fine investment."

"Yes. Growing industry. Suppliers or distributors?"

"Errr... both. Yes, both. The whole industry, sure. I've put quite a few people into gas."

"Interesting," said Andre. "Must look into it. Don't follow the industry. Steel is my baby."

"That so?"

Andre nodded. "Don't be fooled by the softness in the steels. Basically, steel is sound."

"That so? I've got people short in steels."

"Risky." Andre flicked the gold chain at his vest. "That's all I'll say. Know Toledo Steel?"

"A minor producer," said Bill.

"Special situation." Andre lowered his voice though no one was near them. "Big capital program just completed. Insiders buying. I've got plenty myself. Watch TS."

"That so?" Bill made a mental note to investigate the company. His research department had condemned the steels and the stocks had been lagging lately. But one never knew in this business. Tips came from here and there and most of them were as phony as a three dollar bill. Still, some worked. He could not trust Andre, of course, but the stock market was their profession; it would be unethical for him to lie about that.

They found Marsha dancing with a fellow whose tousled hair fell over his right eye. When the song ended she approached them, followed by her partner.

"Mercer I want you to meet Bill Meyers and Andre Blaine," she said. "This is Mercer Hastings. Mercer is writing a novel of the open road."

"Like Tobacco Road?" quipped Bill.

"No, it's about motorcycling through the United States," she added. "Isn't that right?"

"Yeah, you got it." Mercer yanked her arm so that she faced him. Andre stiffened, and Bill was annoyed at the possessive attitude of both the newcomer and his more established rival.

"Let's blow this joint," Mercer said, loud enough for all of them to hear. "I've got my rod downstairs. We can be a million miles from nowhere in no time."

"Can't." Marsha smiled sweetly. "My fiancé wouldn't approve." She pointed at Andre.

Despite his shock, Bill said, "yeah, it wouldn't be cricket and all that jazz."

"Nobody asked you, Cary Grant." Mercer's left upper lip curled in a snarl. He surveyed Andre from head to toe, then turned to Marsha with a sigh of disbelief. "Okay. It's your funeral." He walked away.

"I ought to clout that lug," said Andre, without moving to follow him.

"I wouldn't," said Bill. "Those bulges in his corduroy shirt weren't pads. Besides, congratulations on your engagement."

"I had to say something," said Marsha quickly.

"Did you mean it?" asked Andre.

"I had to get rid of him," she replied.

"You could have said you had leprosy," suggested Ann.

"He'd have thought her irresistible then," said Bill.

"Marsha, I must speak to you," said Andre, "privately."

"Whoa now, wait a minute. Marsha's my date tonight." Bill swept her into the middle of the room before anyone could reply.

"What's going on here?" he asked as they danced. "Are you serious about Andy boy?"

"Jealous?"

"Nooooo. Yes, by God, I am," he exclaimed.

"You're not serious about me, and Andre is."

"Why jump to conclusions? I am serious. I mean, well, that's unfair to put me on the spot."

"Sorry."

"I'll bet you are," he said sarcastically. "I don't like the gleam in Andy's eye – like a pitchman about to peddle a used car. Promise you won't be serious with him tonight. This is our date, remember?"

She did not answer and the music stopped; Andre took her for the next dance. Bill spotted a pretty girl, her blonde hair tied in a bun, and he toyed with the idea of approaching her. But then he might become involved and lose Marsha. No, a bird in hand... was the surest policy tonight.

"Why can't all girls be as uncomplicated as you," he said to Ann.

"Don't kid yourself," she replied. "I have complications."

The music ended abruptly and somebody announced that the entertainment would begin in the next room. Everyone jammed in, piling on the bed, grabbing the few chairs and then filling the floor. "Bet they never sweep in this house," muttered Bill. The entertainment turned out to be folk singing, led by the guitarist they had seen earlier. After two songs Bill urged Marsha to leave with him. She wanted to stay but he persisted.

"I've done what you wanted," he said, "now it's your turn." She consented, finally, and they bade goodbye to their friends to the accompaniment of numerous "shushes." Andre's sad eyes betrayed his apparent concern. Bill pumped his hand several times.

"Whew," Bill puffed as they started downstairs. "Now to my place to exhale this nonsense. No originality in parties anymore."

As soon as they entered his apartment Bill set up the long playing record, "Tangoes to Love By," to be followed by "Cha-cha Passion," a Pepe Pope recording. He asked if she had heard the "Passion" before and she said she had. "That music really moves." he said. He returned from the kitchenette with two scotches, ice, a jug of water and the bottle. Marsha lounged in an armchair. He placed the tray on the sofa table and invited her to sit beside him. She did. Then he shut the main lights.

"Glaring lights," he said, shaking his head, "bad for the eyes."

They sipped their drinks. When he attempted to kiss her she turned her head and he landed on her cheek.

"Strike one," he said.

"Strike five is coming up," she snapped.

"Just like a woman. Only three strikes allowed and she wants five." He gulped his drink and lit a cigarette. He made another pass but she pushed him away.

"You don't seem to realize that I'm nearly married," she said.

"What! You're not even engaged to that guy. And if you know what's good for you, you won't be."

"Do you know what's good for me?"

"Sure I do."

"What?"

"Me, that's what, yours truly William P. Meyers."

"You never mentioned your middle name. See, I don't know anything about you. What is it?"

"Pershing."

"Strong sound." She giggled. "The general?"

"Un-huh. My father admired him."

"Why do you think you'd be better for me than Andre?"

"Because we go together, like steak and red wine."

"Who's the steak?"

"Don't interrupt. You and Andy boy, that's combining red meat and white wine. By themselves they're fine, but not together."

"I guess I'm the steak."

"That doesn't matter. It's the combination that counts."

He whispered in her ear. "We're the right combination, honey, can't you tell?" He kissed her neck and tried to reach her lips. But she resisted stiffly.

"What's the matter?" he exclaimed. "Wait. Don't answer. Uncle Willie knows. You've been guzzling cheap wine and you've barely touched your first little scotchy." He handed her a glass and grasped his.

"I can drink like a fish," she said.

"Don't threaten. Just take your medicine."

When they finished, Bill poured two more. By taunting her to match him, they quickly consumed the second round and began a third. He used double shots each time, finally emptying the bottle.

"You pour that stuff like you owned the company," she said.

"Wow. Never thought of that. All the damn liquor I down and I don't own a single distillery share. Very sharp of you to mention it. See what I mean about the right combination? Another chick would never think of that."

She laughed. "It's not difficult when you go out with two stock brokers."

The tangoes had subsided and the cha-chas taken over. The strong repetitive rhythm seemed to signal his loins and a warm blissful glow spread through his body. He cuddled up to her, feeling suddenly silly and gay and affectionate. He crooned, "now kiss me, kiss me, kiss me baby, just like you always done before."

Marsha sat upright. "You've had enough Mr. Meyers."

"What the hell's happened between us?" he bellowed. "Don't you remember the last time. There!" He pointed to the bearskin crumpled on the floor. "That was us, you and me, and it was great!"

As he ejaculated the last words the thought flashed through his fuzzy brain that perhaps he had been an awkward lover. Oh Christ, he groaned inwardly, that was it. He'd flubbed the dub. His technique had been faulty; she hadn't enjoyed it. Oh nuts. It was inexcusable; she was perfectly right in giving him a hard time now. And that bald headed son-of-a-bitch Blaine was probably as cool as a cucumber.

"That night," he breathed. "I'm sorry if I didn't... if you didn't...."

"What?"

"I may have been too exciting. ...err, excited" he said, turning away and feeling that if she stabbed him in the chest at that moment he could not really blame her.

"That's not it at all."

"Well, what's wrong then?" he demanded, brightening.

"You can't expect us to do that all the time."

"But you can't turn back the clock either."

"Why not?" She seemed surprised. "No law against it. We flip the clock forward and backward for daylight saving time. Why can't we do it any other time?"

"Just isn't done," he said weakly, trying to focus.

"That's no excuse. The world would be much improved if we turned the clock backward or forward whenever we wanted to. I definitely believe that."

"I don't get your point, honey?"

"Ever heard of Zen? It's an oriental religion. I had a course in school once and Zen was included.... I wish I had a blackboard. Do you have some paper? No, never mind. Imagine that time is relative; there is no special time but it's all a flowing river. And we're all in the flow, see? Now, the last time I was here we moved the clock forward. We acted as if we had known each other for ages and ages and were in love or engaged or married. But we weren't. See? We moved the future into the present. But it worked out. You didn't seem to mind at all."

"I wasn't watching the clock," he said.

"All the same, we did. Together. Okay, no harm's done. We feel fine. But now we set the clock back again. This way we're not slaves to time and the way things go. It's exciting."

He slid lower in the sofa, suddenly exhausted. "A philosopher. No wonder I don't dig you half the time."

Her lips parted and her even teeth were gleaming in the dull light. "You understand me very well William Pershing Meyers."

"And hard as nails, as steel. Can't sell you short."

"Did you want to?" She touched his face.

"No," he said, rousing himself. "An idle thought…. A philosopher with curves… I never expected it."

"Mind?"

"Guess not." He embraced her slowly.

"Life would be dull if we knew all the answers," she said.

"We won't be dull," he said emphatically. "Will we? Ever?"

She kissed him full on the lips; then she made him take her home.

Chapter 14

The party was breaking up. The dancing had ended; the phonograph, several played records inside, was neglected; the folk singing was done, the liquor gone, and aside from the couples huddled in corners, conversing in whispers, the movement was toward the door. Ann was saying goodbye to some friends when Cowels offered to accompany her home.

"You don't have to, Stan, really, it's close by," she said, offering her hand as a parting gesture. He clasped it firmly and held on. "But I want to dear Ann," he said. "It would be a great pleasure for me. Besides, I'm leaving too."

She did not argue and he followed her downstairs.

"I couldn't leave you unguarded in our corrupt city streets at this hour," he continued, resuming his familiar bantering tone. "Do you peruse my copy, Ann dearest, sometimes, do you?

"...the assaults upon innocent maidens like yourself as they stroll along, fondling their rosary beads perhaps, a prayer book or some flowers in one hand. The night prowlers wait for them in the dark places where the street lamp has been broken. The sex fiends, ugh… the next day… terrible, terrible. I steel myself to write such stories."

"All right Sir Lancelot, thanks for being considerate."

She slapped him on the back playfully. "Ohhh," he exclaimed, ""your touch… what was it?… the caress of a blade." She looked at him in the glow of the street lights and his solemnity shattered into laughter. He took her hand and they ran along the deserted sidestreet. "Hurry up, your mother will be furious," he said.

"Wait." She pulled off her high-heeled shoes and took his hand again and they ran, a broken skipping pace.

"You're crazy Cowels," she said, panting, and pulling him to a halt. "I'm home."

"Let me come up," he said.

"Too late Cowels…ohhh… nearly two." She feigned shock. "What would mother say?"

"Don't tell her…. It was so short, Ann dear. We're never alone. You suspect me… I know, but…."

She interrupted, "I trust you Stan. We're… teammates, aren't we? But it's terribly late…."

"I want to talk to you," he said.

"Not tonight. It's too late, and it's not right either, is it? Is it Cowels?"

He did not answer. Their eyes met in the semi-darkness of the outer hallway. His hands reached out and touched her shoulders; he seemed taller, more imposing in the dimness; his hair was like the white cap of a huge wave.

"It's not right Cowels, you know it." She turned her back to him fumbling in her handbag for the key to the main entranceway. She opened the door and went in. Cowels did not move. She held the door open.

"What will you drink Mr. Cowels?" She laughed and tossed her handbag on the sofa.

"Since you ask, Miss Rawley, I'd like a cool limpid wine." He sat on the sofa.

"I have it," she said, going to the refrigerator. "I'm sure it's cool. It's been in here awhile. May be limp instead of limpid." She brought out two glasses and the wine and sat beside him.

"But I'm not limp," she continued, pouring the wine.

"We grow strong out West. Do you think you can overpower me? You can't. I'm terribly strong. Feel." She flexed her arm and he held it like a hotcake fresh from the oven.

"Of course you're strong. I knew you would be. Salud."

They touched glasses and drank.

"Crazy party, wasn't it? So many things at once. Not as nice as my party. Did you like mine better?"

"Sure. I like everything about you better. You're straight, you're unspoiled, you're an honest dame in a phony town. A rarity." He smiled and lifted his glass to her.

"Am I? Do you really think so, or is this part of your line? Guys use so many lines. I'm not special though. Not at all. I can't figure out why you're interested in me. Why me?"

"Because you're real. A real person. I've seen enough glass to tell a real gem, and a pretty and sweet one, too."

"Cut it out. Here, fill your glass." She refilled hers.

"You're wrong Cowels. I'm just like all the others, except maybe a little stupider. At least in this town. I don't understand how people think here, girls or guys. Guess I'm still a hick. But I appreciate your compliments. Thanks."

He leaned toward her slowly; her nostrils flared and she tensed. He kissed her nose. Her eyes softened and became a trifle liquid; they laughed.

"Turn off the lamp behind you," she said.

"Can't you bear to look at me?"

"Turn it off. Be good." He did.

"See, it's not really dark now. There's a lamppost outside that throws a light in here all night, a little light."

He embraced her gently but she flung her arms around his neck and pressed her mouth to his; then she broke away. "Why me Cowels?" It was a cry.

"Words are careless," he whispered. "They hide meanings."

She rested her head against his shoulder and curled herself like a huge cat so that the beginnings of her knees lay on his lap. "I'm tired; it's so late." She yawned. "Why aren't you Jack Stopple? He should be here now, not you. I can't get involved with you Cowels. We're not meant for each other; we're out of balance."

"Do you really think everything would be right if Jack were here?"

"Yes. Don't you? Can't you see us together?"

"Oh, it's possible, anything's possible. It's a strange world and at one time or another almost anything goes. Even you and Jack."

"You're kidding. You see yourself and me but not Jack and me? I wonder. But no matter. Want a cigarette?" They lit up and refilled their glasses with wine.

"Cowels, want to stay up all night and smoke and drink and talk?"

"I'll tell you the mournful tale of my life and you'll weep for sorrow for me and by daybreak...."

"I'll hate your guts," she said. "All right, begin. You said you wanted to talk, now tell me about the wife that didn't understand you and things like that."

"It's not an off-color joke, little girl. Don't be so smart; think you've heard everything?"

"I've heard a few stories," she said. "I'm from Reno, remember?"

He smiled. "But you've been sheltered."

"My Pop runs a hotel. So I've had company under the shelter. I'll tell you about me. Not too exciting, but then I'm still young.... Oh I'm sorry. Didn't mean anything by that, really."

She leaned back on the sofa and stretched her arms; her eyes were glassy. "I was in love with a boy. We grew up together, lived in the same street, same age, same class. He loved me too; that was understood, like you said before, without words but with the meaning clear.... Except I suppose it wasn't so clear.... Words are important too, because without words there are only feelings and feelings can be so vague and complicated. Nobody ever feels what another feels. Words can bridge the gap.

"But we didn't need words because everything was so natural: our families were friends and we went to the same church and even our fathers had business dealings together. We went steady in college, the University of Nevada, that's in Reno, you know, a small campus but pretty. Then the Korean War came along and he was drafted. He went overseas and we wrote lots of letters. Then his letters stopped and I heard he had been wounded. I said I'd wait for him and it didn't matter. He got better in Japan; then he wrote he was re-enlisting and staying in Japan and his letters came less. His folks were worried; they said he had a Japanese girl friend. Then I heard he had married her."

She lit another cigarette from the one she had smoked down. "I didn't believe it; I think everybody kinda doubted, even his parents. Then one day his mother told me he was coming home, with his wife, and a son. Then I believed it. I didn't want to be around when he got back. I didn't think I could take it. Might have embarrassed him too. Reno isn't such a big town, you know, not the permanent population. Anyway, I wanted to get away and my father understood. So here I am in New York."

Cowels appeared to be thinking about something else.

"Did New York help?" he asked.

"Funny. In New York I feel closer to Reno than I ever did when I lived there. The people there, the streets, everything is more real to me than New York. Ever been there?"

"No. My wife was."

"Oh. Well, underneath the divorce and the gambling is a regular small town life. In fact the Reno people are kinda prudish you might say, or simple minded. It's as if two towns existed side by side. Sometimes the Reno people mix with the out-of-towners, just for the laughs, but they always come back to earth."

She sighed and ran her hands through her hair. "My coming to New York must be like a stranger entering Harold's Club. It's a weird world with lots of written and unwritten rules of games. Takes a while to learn them. And you need luck…. Say, you're usually the gabby one and now you're in a church."

"Just thinking how fine it is to be alive at this hour and to be drinking cool limp wine. My glass is empty, have you noticed my dear?"

She snuggled deeper into the sofa. "I'm so comfortable here," she said. "Help yourself. You're not so feeble."

"Ann Rawley. I may be a gray-haired has-been, but I'm only 39 years old, so stop insinuating I'm the twin of Methuselah."

He poured the last of the bottle into his glass. "I really am 39, not a Jack Benny 39. Ten years ago I was a hot-shot reporter in this town. Much hotter than your dream boy Jack Stopple. I didn't work for I.N. then; no, not that meat packer. I was with the Blade, and a nosier newshound you couldn't find. Wasn't a decent scandal in this berg I didn't whiff."

He gulped at his drink and a puff of air escaped his lungs immediately afterward. "You may not remember Mayor Haley, a colorful character but as corrupt a politician as this city has known, and this city has known a few. The Blade was after Haley and it was my pleasant task to uncover the garbage can so that all of the fair citizens of this metropolis could have a stiff smell. I got plenty of bylines then and top money too, much higher than union scale. There was graft in school construction, and roads, political payoffs and police bribery and organized prostitution and all the involved links ended at city hall. Stanley P. Cowels broke a lot of it. With the help of several state commissions and others interested in Haley's scalp. But the tie-in with Haley could never be proven. Eventually we got him, though. And that's a story that never got printed, though there were plenty of hints in the gossip columns. Haley had a mistress and she turned out to be the wife of a local banker. It was dynamite and the Blade had the goods on him, even a picture, but it wasn't necessary to use it. Haley knew the jig was up. He didn't run for re-election; retired from politics, took his bundle up to Montreal, where he's practicing law."

Cowels paced the floor, his empty glass in hand. "I was damn busy all during the Haley battle. Plenty of night work; often I couldn't get out to the house in Freeport for days. Of course, the overtime was piling up and the dough coming in nicely. My wife said she understood; she knew being a newsman's wife sometimes can be like a country doctor's. But she had two kids to take care of... I did neglect her. Didn't realize it then, or if I did I thought it would be temporary. I was hustling for her and the kids and us. I thought I was....

"When she suggested a divorce I laughed. Joke of the year. When I knew it wasn't a joke, it took the wind outta me. It was rather funny, I suppose, if one can be objective; a silly joke that life plays when we're cutting down others and thinking we're immune somehow.... This guy... he was a salesman, yes, a door-to-door salesman... siding or roofing or some crap like that. I suppose he just knocked at our door, at random, and my wife let him in... the roof was thin in spots.... Thin... Imagine, he was sitting in my parlor, selling roofing and himself while I was sweating in the damn subway or in some smoky press room...."

"You don't have to tell me," said Ann.

"No," insisted Cowels. "I want to... Funny, I never dreamed my wife would prefer a roofing salesman to a top-flight reporter like me. But then he was there, and I wasn't. So that was the twist. Anyway, she was smarter than I thought. I was due for both barrels, but I didn't know it yet. She got the divorce in Reno, your sweet little countryfolk town. I didn't fight it. She didn't ask for money or even the children. So I had no kick.... They went to Texas I heard, and this roofing guy has made out there; a regular businessman he is.... A pal on a San Antonio daily keeps me informed....

"Enough Stan," said Ann, beckoning to him. "Forget it."

"Oh I can't forget it, honey, no no I'll never forget it. My little souvenir and I can't toss it away. Well, I got two fine sons and my mother helps me with them, so I'm not so bad off. There's worse I know... But you ought to know the rest, there's not much more... just at this time, Mayor Haley decides it's wiser to retire and skip the country and Stanley P. Cowels is left without a whipping boy. I was making damn good money then, double most on the Blade. Well, with Haley gone I'm back on the city beat and the Blade management discovers I'm a pretty high-priced leg man.

So one day the boss says my salary is being chopped from $200 a week to $95; that was the top union minimum then. I told him to shove it. Hell, I had a reputation in this town and I figured I could do better elsewhere. I guess I wasn't thinking too clearly then; my marriage breaking up didn't help. Anyway, I quit and started making the rounds. Then I discovered some more facts of life; that there are hundreds of guys begging for every opening and most of them would work for less than the minimum, just to get a break on a New York paper. And with Haley gone, my fine reputation wasn't worth a subway token. They even linked me with the Haley mess, figured I'd been in on the graft and that was the reason I had separated from the Blade... It was a tough lesson but I finally learned it. When I came off my cloud I was able to find a job, with I.N., ending up on rewrite. Actually I preferred it to mixing with the guys on the beats who knew me in better days. So I retired, you might say, put on an aged beatnik front and started pinching copy girls. Funny story, huh?"

"Is that why your hair turned gray?"

"No, darling." He chuckled. "It runs in the family."

Ann closed her eyes and huddled into the sofa and waited. Cowels observed the smoke curling up from his cigarette like a lazy python.

"I'll go now," he said.

"Don't you want to stay?" Her eyes had opened and her voice showed surprise and some disappointment.

"Yes. But I'd better not. Besides, my sons come into my room in the mornings, usually. They might not understand my not being home."

"Oh... Okay papa. Thanks for taking me home."

She kissed him at the door.

127

Chapter 15

For the first time in many months, Sylvia felt rather contented. She still had unpleasant moments when for no apparent cause she became irritable and nervous, when she wanted to junk everything and say to hell with everybody and flee the city for no place in particular. But these feelings came less frequently and their intensity had weakened to the point where she could control herself without difficulty.

She smoked less, too, and it was not only because Jack disapproved of smoking but because she seemed to have lost her craving for tobacco. She was pleased also to discover that she needed no coffee-break during the workday; she could concentrate for hours on a copy or layout assignment. Once the office had emptied without her being distracted and the sudden realization of her new found power of concentration was a joy and an excitement.

Realistically, she credited Jack for her new well-being, but with equal frankness she decided that she did not love him. She felt rather guilty about this; not regarding Jack in particular, but because she knew she had never been in love. She felt instinctively that she might be unable to love, that something was lacking in her, or that something had been killed. But she no longer brooded over this. She did have Jack and he was good for her and if she was not overpowered with yearnings for him, if she suffered no loss of appetite, if she was not distracted, if, on the contrary, she was more than ever in control of herself, then so much the better.

At first she believed she had given in to him too quickly. Nobody values what they get easily. But he had wanted her, needed her, and she had wanted him. She had never been a coquette. She had wondered if he would drop her immediately after his success. Some men were funny that way: little boys really, interested only in little conquests. But Jack had not quit her. As the days and weeks slipped by he grew more tender, more affectionate, and his warmth, she knew, was partly responsible for her new self-confidence.

She enjoyed strolling with him in Central Park or down Fifth Avenue, feeling his forearm stiffen as she grasped it and knowing, secretly, that this was more than a mere reflex. She recalled with pleasure when she first learned of the possibility of power over a man. Petting with her high school beau – they were only children – in the back seat of a car: how wonderful when he twitched and heaved and she suspected that she had caused it. When she touched him in certain ways he became agitated, his breath came fast and short like a dog's; if she touched him other ways he became almost helpless, weak as if drugged. At his moment of passion he would cry out," "I love you so much."

Jack had said the same thing. How unoriginal men were. When she was alone and naked with Jack it took her utmost control to refrain from fondling him; she wanted to caress his breasts the way he did hers, run the tips of her fingers down his chest and along the ripples of his stomach, flitting down his muscular thighs and legs. But she held back; he would have been shocked at her forwardness, as other men had, and imagined she was too professional, something dirty and to be disrespected. Why did men insist women be virginal in spirit if not in fact?

But there was a rule of the game and wisely, she thought, she permitted him to be the aggressor.

Jack had a feminine aspect, she thought, a certain sensitivity that she associated with women. Upright and handsome, gabbing in his dreamy philosophical manner, making so much sense sometimes, or so much nonsense, he could tell when she had stopped listening. A line would deepen in his forehead and his mouth would narrow in a frown and the indentation of his chin would somehow be more pronounced. His face expressed his every emotion, it seemed, and by now she felt she could read the lines and depressions like a roadmap. But he was seldom moody or irritable and when he turned that way she found she was able to bring him out of it with a few words or a simple gesture. For he had an excellent ability to be objective about himself, to laugh at his mannerism: a refreshing contrast to the self-occupation and seriousness of most men.

She had not abandoned her feature project. But she felt ashamed for having tried, like a headstrong general, to overwhelm the fortress frontally, unmindful of the losses. Why storm a fortification that can be encircled or bypassed? Science had finally demonstrated that the shortest distance between points was not the obvious straight line but the subtle curve, something that strategists in love and war had recognized for ages.

If Jack waited for her to broach the subject again, Sylvia purposely removed the pressure so completely that it created a void. He would have to take the initiative; when he had, tentatively, she had tactfully retreated. He was only testing her, but she was in no hurry. The Jeff H. feature was her pet, without a deadline, and it would be as effective in a month or two as now.

Her withdrawal of the feature project gave rise to another idea: to remove all pressures. She would create a complete vacuum. (Science could teach so much about human relations, if only we heeded.) She made him the boss; more than that, she appeared his slave. She let him initiate every idea and action. She refused to argue, but capitulated immediately. She asked his advice continually and gave the impression that she followed it unquestioningly. She asked his permission in the most trivial matters ("Do you mind if I take a cigarette?" "May we look into this shop window?") She watched with secret glee the wonder in his face when she agreed that "public relations was rarely in the public interest." Undoubtedly women had employed such tactics to survive the centuries when they lacked independence, weaving an illusion of surrender to conquer subtly. How many battles would have been won by women generals? (Joan of Arc had behaved like a man, only to receive a man's reward.)

Yet Sylvia did not believe she was only playing a sly game. She cared for Jack and though she wanted to be completely independent and was, in fact, self-sufficient, she recognized that she needed him. She hated to admit it, but she did. Was it really him, the complete person, that she wanted, or only his throbbing instrument that could tickle her into a semi-insanity until nothing mattered? What a farce to contemplate! Was she dependent, ultimately, after all her effort and will and intelligence on a stubby pink rod so much like a dime-store soldier?

Of course, she could stimulate herself; she had learned to do that. So, in a sense, she could be self-sufficient in sex, too. But it was not the same as having a man. Not that any man would do for her. Some were so clumsy, so stupid, that sex with them was a bore; others were too clever, too knowing in the intricacies, but lacking in the essential spontaneity, that undefinable imaginative spark that shaded knowledge and removed sex from the contrived.

She recalled the first man who had taken her, raped her actually, one rainy afternoon when the family was out. An older man, her father's best friend; he said he wanted to be her friend too. She had just celebrated her eighteenth birthday. No matter. She had been terribly frightened but she remembered not resisting. She had wanted to know, and she found out. Now, it was no longer frightening. But occasionally it was disturbing. Strange, that when sex was most pleasing it was also most upsetting. As with Jack. She enjoyed the petting and the play and she could relax and not fear it. But suddenly she would feel herself losing control, becoming maddeningly helpless to her surging body and her wild emotions and the man who possessed her. She hated these moments; they came like a nightmare; she would twist and strain, fighting to hold on to her will, to hold on, to hold on…. She gave her mouth, her arms, her legs, her breasts, she surrendered her body, but he would not be satisfied. He was an insatiable monster wanting more and more, everything, all, she was suffocating, dying…. Sometimes, against her judgment, against her will, battling all the way, she was forced into a blazing moment of destruction when the universe exploded with rockets and lightening and shattering silence and heaven and hell merged and disappeared in a sizzle. Then there was nothingness for a long, long moment as if she had died; the blissful peace of unfeeling and sometimes sleep. A terrible experience, but miraculous and fascinating as only terrible experiences can be. They did not happen often. Fortunately. But Jack was one who could bring her to this brink of chaos; he had the spirit, the dangerous proficiency. She wondered if it was learned or a natural talent, like playing the piano without lessons, or being able to draw, untrained and yet with sensitivity and beauty. Or did she bring some power out of him, some mystery that only she could inspire? So Jack had became a wonder to her, pleasantly strange and exciting and dangerous. She had to exert tremendous self-control at times or she found herself wanting to marry him. She did want to marry, but not someone like Jack. He might, in time, destroy her, make a tool of her, a total dependent, an insignificant bourgeois housewife who would find satisfaction in polishing furniture and cooking and rearing children and waiting impatiently for night when he would sleep with her. She had no plans for such a life. That might have done for her mother, and perhaps millions of other females. But not for her. She would marry somebody, but she would surrender herself to no man.

Or to no woman either. It had happened once in a summer camp for "underprivileged" children and had cured her of any notions along that line. How happy her mother had been when the social agency selected little Sylvia Perini (her name before she changed it to Parker) for two weeks away from the heat of their Brooklyn tenement into what the brochure described as "the wholesome atmosphere of the countryside." Like so many sheep, they were loaded on a bus and most of the girls bawled. But not Sylvia. She was neither sad, nor frightened, nor happy. Miss Gray, the agency mistress, perhaps was impressed by her impassivity. She made her a cabin leader in camp, a squad leader in evening formation. She remembered how the woman, tall and angular, would touch her when she spoke, always courteously. But adults had abused her often that way, pinching her like a rag doll. She hated it but had learned to ignore it.

Then one afternoon she cut her leg playing softball. It was a superficial wound, only a scratch, but Miss Gray insisted on applying first aid. She had been rather startled in the cabin when Miss Gray stroked her leg. "You're sure there's nothing broken," she had asked, her hand going up and down, softly, reaching higher on the warm inside of her thigh. "I'm fine," she had replied, and ran out. Then, on the overnight hike, in the shadows of thick pines, underneath a darkening sky, amidst strange hoots and unseen rustlings, she had been happy when Miss Gray suggested they combine their blankets into a single bed. Later, in the blackness she awoke to feel the woman's hands caressing her, slipping inside her undergarments. She thought Miss Gray was moving in her sleep and she turned on her side. But then she heard a whisper, "Don't awaken the others," and felt moist lips upon her belly and legs. She wanted to scream but was too scared. In the morning Miss Gray made her promise never to tell anyone what had happened, because nobody would believe her. She had never told. But neither had she ever desired a repetition.

Jack invited her to a Broadway show; they went to the ballet and once to a performance of "Madame Butterfly" at the Metropolitan Opera; they went to the arty little cinemas; both enjoyed the thin but lively British comedies. But more often he would call her, or Sylvia would phone him at home or at work and they would meet at a restaurant or a street corner or their apartments. On Sundays they often drove into the countryside of Long Island or New Jersey; they would take sandwiches and lunch at a grassy spot. Often, on weekday evenings, while most New Yorkers scurried toward the subways, they would stroll to the Central Park zoo seeking the tiger from Siam, a favorite now, like a pet cat. Later they would dine at the zoo's cafeteria, sitting on the terrace eating hot soup and leafy salads with salted crackers, tossing crumbs to the pigeons.

She came to his apartment without pretense, as if nothing could be more natural, and if it was not too hot they cooked dinner together: she preparing the salad (she had a passion for them) and he broiling lamb chops or steak (they agreed on medium rare). Afterward, in his long white baker's apron, she washed the dishes while he wiped and put them away. Usually the radio was tuned to concert music. Invariably, when she came to his place, they would end by undressing and going to bed. They would do that naturally, too, without coaxing. He would look at her seriously, lovingly; they would embrace.

He might unfasten the top buttons of her sweater or blouse and slip his hand underneath. She would let him, leaning her head on his shoulder, sometimes kissing his neck. At one point he would lower the shades and shut the lights, except for the bath room light, so that there was a glow in the room but no brightness. They would undress, folding their clothes neatly on the easy chair or in the closet. He kept extra hangers. Then, her pale flesh reflecting dimly the bathroom light so that she seemed like a lithe marble statue, she would lift the coverlet and ease underneath, extending her limbs, allowing her head to sink softly into the foam-rubber pillow. Soon he would follow, naked too, except for his socks.

To Jack it was a comfortable affair, strangely wonderful and unexpected. The friction between them had vanished, as if rocketing skyward they had suddenly left the murky atmosphere for the thin tranquility beyond. There was something ideal between them now, Jack thought, like a dream. But like a dream, it seemed so fragile and tenuous that he feared he must awaken someday unable to recall the details. There was no pact, nothing spoken, but their understanding seemed the stronger for its lack of formality. When he held her in his arms and felt her firm flesh, so much like that of a young athlete, yield against his, he could not doubt the reality of their love. And yet, because she made no demands, because she neither asked nor seemed to expect anything, because whatever he offered was sufficient, he was puzzled and vaguely nervous.

To whatever he suggested she invariably acquiesced. If her idea differed, she abandoned it at his first objection. She never complained, even when her taste seemed obviously opposed to his. "Well, it doesn't matter," she would say, or "It's the same to me," or "You're right, I hadn't thought of that." Yet the more she agreed, the more she bowed to his will, the more agitated he became. He could understand neither her nor himself. The experience was too new. His affairs before had been fiery or tumultuous or simply annoying, but never tranquil. And yet this was what he always knew love, real love, would be like. Natural. Easy. Casual. Without effort.

He talked more about journalism and publicity and his work and hers. He gave his opinions on politics and plays and modern art and he demanded hers. When they paralleled his, he was both glad and disappointed. He discussed the concept of progress and "getting ahead" and he waited for her to mention the Jeff H. account and the feature story. But she never did. He became impatient and asked what had became of the copy she had shown him weeks ago. "It's still in the works," she replied, and changed the subject. She was everything he wanted, everything every man dreams of: a woman completely akin to his nature; and still he yearned.

He decided to provoke her. He would condemn publicity, public relations and all advertising as frauds. "Utterly wasteful of human resources," he would say, "deceitful occupations, inducing innocents to buy what they did not want, did not need and what often harmed them mentally, morally, physically and spiritually." Publicity cajoled people to pawn their futures, making them servants to their auto loans, installment-bought washing machines, yes, and their miracle-promising body-building schemes. An honest man or woman would sell his body sooner than his self-respect in such a field. The whole advertising apparatus should be scrapped and its performers put to work in factories producing something useful for society.

He prepared for a battle that would climax with namecalling and curses and the straining of their relationship to the breaking point. And then – he had planned well – at the crucial moment, when everything between them was about to collapse, he would fold her in his arms. She would resist, yes, he was prepared for that. He wanted that. But he would force her. No matter how she twisted and squirmed and cried he would hold her; employing all his strength, he would embrace and smother her with kisses. As she struggled in his arms, her movements becoming weaker, he would say that whatever they argued about was of no consequence because their love was real and lasting, the only important thing in the whole jumbled universe. He would caress her hair and kiss her softly, gently; then he would carry her to bed. Perhaps she would still resist; so much the better. He would take her, lift her in his arms like a dear child and lay her lovingly upon the white sheets. He would remove her clothing, piece by piece, caressing and kissing her all the while, and then he would love her. She would feel his weight and his force and she would know him.

But like a puff of pink sugar candy, his plan melted to nothing. He played his part well, he thought. His vehemence surprised him; his breath came gaspy at the end. But she did not swallow the bait; she did not seem in the least offended and even laughed and said she did not realize he felt so strongly. Without a trace of rancor, she discussed public service advertising: how worthy causes were sponsored as well as those less worthy. Advertising made people lift their sights and standards of living, she said, but this did them no harm and was essential for the progress of society. Besides, there were too many factory workers already and how were all the factory products to be sold without advertising.

Jack had the uneasy impression that she was tolerantly lecturing her angry little boy.

Afterward, they went to bed. He had possessed her, not the way he wanted to, with his heart raging with the excitement of lust and conquest. They made love calmly, matter-of-factly, until the final moments, of course. There was a flurry then. She seemed to enjoy herself and him and he was happy, afterward, despite his vague moodiness.

As time passed Jack became accustomed to Sylvia's behavior. She was subordinating herself to him because she loved him. And this realization inspired a greater love in him for her. He felt honored by her understanding of him and grateful for the gift of herself and he desired to do things for her. He gave himself physically but he enjoyed their sexual relationship so much that he felt he was giving nothing that he was not taking doublefold. He brought her flowers and small gifts but he felt these were not enough; they did not express him.

One evening he asked to see the Jeff H. feature story again. He wanted to reread it, if she did not object. Though she seldom referred to her work anymore, Jack decided it was because he had voiced such strong objections to it. Nevertheless he knew it consumed much of her energy and most of her time. Often she worked past five o'clock and occasionally when he picked her up at her office, it was otherwise deserted. Helping her with this feature would be something distinctive that he could do. And he would do it voluntarily; it would be his special gift. Taking credit for her initiative no longer troubled him, nor did the publicity aspect. A story was a story; the source did not matter. Many news features were rewrites of publicity releases. As for the Jeff H. plug, it fit the piece and would be obvious only to whom it was important.

Going over the copy again he realized it needed less altering than he had imagined earlier. Sylvia was right; the technicalities would only clutter the message. With a gimmick lead, a quote or two, it would be as good a feature as I.N. generally used. He asked if it were still uncommitted and if he could rework it for his wire service. When she replied that he could do what he liked with it he was overjoyed.

He angled the copy by quoting a prominent heart surgeon on the importance of exercise to proper coronary action. Everybody's heart crazy these days, he mused; that should sell it. For a trick lead, he cited a heart patient's amazement when ordered by his physician to exercise. He rewrote several paragraphs, sharpening the sentences, adding a few details. He thought he improved, finally, the Jeff H. plug. It was completed in two nights. When he read the revised copy to Sylvia and declared he would submit it to his boss tomorrow he was strangely exhilarated.

Chapter 16

The telephone's jangle awakened Jack shortly before five the next morning. Walker, on the I.N. "lobster trick," ordered him to Broadway and 75th street: a clothing store fire threatened an apartment house.

"Make it fast," he said. "You can grab a cab."

"Thanks pal," answered Jack. The phone clicked off.

Jack dashed cold water on his face and quickly slipped into his clothes. No time for exercise or food. About to shut the door, he noticed the Jeff H. feature lying neatly on the table. He stuffed it into his inside jacket pocket and jogged downstairs. At the corner he hailed a taxi. Economy-minded I.N. instructed its staffers to use subways and busses, unless told otherwise.

The fire was under control when he arrived but water was still being hosed into the smoking store and the first floor of the building above. Jack located the chief fire officer and got the details. A fireman had been overcome by smoke. Jack got this name and company, the time the blaze began, when it was contained; he verified the address. "How did it start?"

"Undetermined," shouted the fire officer. "Off the record," he said, lowering his voice, "I think business was bad."

Several occupants of the tenement above the store stood in their slippered feet in the street, wrapped in blankets and bathrobes. Jack interviewed two of them; then he obtained a police estimate of the number routed from their flats and the possible damage. After a quarter hour at the scene he telephoned the office.

"Come in and write it," said Walker. "Yeah, take a cab."

Jackson Johns arrived in the office at 11:50 a.m., breathed deeply of the air-conditioned air, rubbed his palms together as if with soap, and ordered a container of coffee. Jack waited until the city editor had finished his coffee before approaching his desk with the feature story. He knew City News would not use it, but to bypass his boss in the chain-of-command might be fatal to the story.

The city editor "hhmmmmmmmmmmed" as he leafed the pages. Suddenly he asked, "how do you spell 'asphyxiate'?"

"Did I use that word?"

"No, no. I merely want you to spell 'asphyxiate'."

Jack did.

"Spell 'atrophy'." Jack did.

"Try 'accommodate'."

Jack spelled it with one m and Mr. Johns, after glancing at a white card on his desk, corrected him. The city editor twisted his head sideways; his eyeglasses slipped down the bridge of his nose. "No excuse for misspelled words Stopple. Words are our hammers and nails. Spelling should have been mastered in grammar school. What school did you go to?"

"Oakland elementary."

"No, no. I meant college. You're a college man, aren't you?"

"Yes, sir. University of California."

"They teach spelling there?"

"I don't think so, Mr. Johns."

"Well, be careful about spelling. I'm glad you came forward today Stopple. Feature stories, well, can't use them here. But I've been meaning to talk to you about your work. Understand you employ a great many commas."

"Oh," replied Jack, mystified.

"Yes." Mr. Johns coughed. "Brought to my attention by one of the copy readers. Commas slow down the story, hamper reader interest. Our stories must be snappy, flow. The reader wants to know over his first coffee, not the refill." He cleared his throat. "Our competitors have been eliminating commas lately and the decision was made upstairs to follow suit."

"I hadn't realized, sir," said Jack.

"It was revealed in memorandum 643, in last week's log." A note of astonishment was in the editor's voice. "Don't you read the log every week?"

"I must have missed the last issue," said Jack.

"The latest issue," corrected Mr. Johns. "Stay with it Stopple. One slip leads to another. You've eliminated your lateness. That's fine. As for your commas, it's not difficult. Cut whenever possible." He leaned forward and put his hand on Jack's arm. "Don't mean to pick on you Jack. But I've got to watch my staff. Upstairs people are watching me. That's the way it goes. So mind your commas now."

"Yes sir. I'll be careful."

"Good." Mr. Johns turned away. Jack waited until the editor became aware of him again. "Yes?"

"About the feature, Mr. Johns."

"I'll send it upstairs. No value here."

A week passed before Jack got word on the story. He had prepared for a longer delay, knowing it would be improper to attempt to rush a decision. But almost to the minute a week later features accepted it.

"We may make a few changes," said a feature editor over the telephone, "but minor ones."

"May I see it before it goes out?" asked Jack.

"Sure. Call you when it's ready."

Pleased with his success, Jack immediately dialed Sylvia's office. But he hung up abruptly. Somebody might overhear the conversation. Beside, features mentioned possible changes, and this could mean dropping the Jeff H. plug.

"I'll do my best to keep it in," he said that evening in Sylvia's apartment.

"I'm sure it will be fine." She threw her arms around his neck and kissed him in a burst of affection. The front door opened.

"Hold it – click, click," said Bill, imitating a cameraman. "That will be all for today. Back on the set at dawn."

They laughed. "Why don't you knock before entering a lady's apartment?" demanded Sylvia, feigning anger.

"But I have my key, honey," said Marsha.

"My girl said that," exclaimed Bill. "Bubbles Golden.'

"Bubbles!" cried Sylvia.

"Yes," said Bill. "Don't you think it suits?"

"I don't like it," said Marsha. "And he won't tell me why he calls me that."

"I will Bubbles, I will."

"There's a fan dancer in Union City called Bubbles something-or-other," mused Jack.

"Don't analyze my pet names friend."

"Let's go out and celebrate," said Jack. "My treat." He encircled Sylvia's waist. "I.N. accepted our story on health and exercise. I'll get a byline, nationwide."

"Wonderful," exclaimed Marsha, beaming at Sylvia who avoided her eyes. Bill pumped his hand. "Great news. We just came from Tony's bar, but we join you in spirit."

As soon as the others departed, Bill clasped Marsha.

"Don't become athletic," she warned.

"Bubbles, you're confusing me with Jack. With me, it's love, the pure unadulterated drug."

"Don't call me that, especially in public. That's a name for a strip teaser."

"Exactly. Bubbles Golden, you're teasing me to death. You're stripping me of my senses. And until you stop I'll retaliate." He kissed her neck and whispered, "come to bed with me. Right now.

They won't be back for an hour at least. Let's jump into bed and forget everything and everybody."

"Bill, I told you we won't do that anymore."

"Honey you can't mean such a terrible thing. You can't halt this great warm flow between us.'

"Yes I can. We can, together. We must control ourselves."

"Maybe you can. Maybe you're made of titanium. But I...."

"What's titanium?"

"A new metal, stronger than steel, and lighter. Big producer is Consolidated Mines, a really cheap stock. Loaded with assets. But that's not what we're discussing now."

"Perhaps it should be. Andre sold me a stock last week and it's already up three points. Why haven't you?"

"Now wait. I refuse to compete with baldy Blaine's prognostications. He's the cause of all our problems. Now I understand. You must drop him."

"But Andre wants to marry me!"

"Sure he does. He's a damn fool."

"What!"

"I mean he's a fool and you shouldn't bother with him. Don't let him confuse you with the stock market. He doesn't know any more than I do. He may guess right, once in a while. But listen, I'm the right one for you. Me. Nobody else. I love you. Don't laugh. I tell you I do. But you're driving me nuts. Now come to bed. Right now."

"No. I said I wouldn't"

"I warn you I won't stand for this. You've no right to use your sex as a weapon against me."

"Why not?"

"If you cared for me, you wouldn't. Marsha, if you won't come to bed I'll... I'll...."

"Do something drastic?" Her eyes opened wide.

"I'll never speak to you again. I'm not fooling."

"You can't mean it. Not if you love me.

"Marsha dear, why won't you understand? I love you so much it's affecting my mind. My work's slipping. The stock market's slipping; everything's going haywire. One of my best customers called me yesterday – Mrs. Flynn. I kept thinking of you; hardly heard what she said. I must have answered "yes dear" and "yes darling." Finally she said, "Mr. William Meyers, all the stock you sold me is down and that deary and darlin' stuff is not gettin' you anyplace." And she canceled her account. See what you're doing to me?"

She rested her hands on his shoulders and he embraced her. "Honey," he whispered; her hair tickled his nose and he brushed it away. "You know I need it – bad."

"I know," she purred.

"Well…."

"What about afterward?"

"After what?" he mooned.

"After you don't need it so bad."

He broke away. "You're laughing at me."

"I'm not even smiling," she said truthfully.

"You're toying with me, like a cat with a mouse!"

She took him in her arms, pressing his head against her cheek. "Do you feel like a mouse?"

"Ahhhh," he screamed. "Monster. Help. You're a monster with a blonde wig."

"And who do you think you are? Little Red Ridinghood?"

"You don't love me … at ALL. You're using me… for amusement!"

"You're not very amusing Mr. Meyers."

"Marsha," he said, straightening himself. "I won't fight with you. I simply refuse. You know how I feel about you. But I won't fight."

"Good," she said.

"I've got to think. About us. I've got to think."

"All right. If you think it's wise."

"What?"

"I think it's wise of you to think," She said, "about us. Think for both of us, Bill. I mean it."

"I will Marsha. Believe me, I will."

Chapter 17

As Marsha clip-clopped down the stone steps of P.S. 91 she heard the short sharp blasts of a powerful automobile horn. Without her eyeglasses she did not immediately recognize the driver. But there was no mistaking the gleaming white Oldsmobile. At the bottom of the stairway she patted two pupils on the cheek and dismissed them. Then she walked to the car.

"Why Andre," she exclaimed, "what are you doing here? Aren't you working today?"

He looked up at her, squinting in the sunlight. "I.... I took off a little early. Want to go for a drive?"

"I've so much to do. It's the end of the term, you know."

"Please Marsha."

She hesitated, arguing silently with his pleading beady eyes. "All right," she said cheerfully.

He jumped out of the car and opened the other door for her. The engine started with a sudden roar; he headed for the Hudson River.

"Why didn't you come?" he asked solemnly.

"Thursday night? I'm awfully sorry Andre. I expected to, I really did, and then something came up at the very last second." She fluffed her hair. "May I use the car mirror?" She tilted the rear-view mirror toward her and lightly combed her hair.

He twisted the mirror back into place when she had finished. "I waited and waited. I called your apartment several times but there was no answer. My mother came over. Unexpected. That topped everything. I didn't want her to be there when you came. I chased her out. Marsha, I chased my own mother out of my house." Anguish reflected in the shrill tones of his voice, but his face remained impassive. "God, at least you could have telephoned."

"I'm sorry Andre. Really I am. I just couldn't get to a telephone."

"Oh."

He turned north into the West Side Highway and they sped along the riverside toward the George Washington bridge. He flipped the radio switch and music came on quickly and loud....

"Hold me, Hug me baby,
Hug me, Hold me baby,
Hold me, Hug me baby,
Bay-bee, Hug meeeee."

Andre lowered the volume and turned his head slightly toward her, keeping his eyes on the road.

"Strange that you couldn't get to a telephone," he said, "Here I was waiting and ...."

"Oh, stop harping on that," she interrupted.

"...Hug me. Hold me baby,
Hold me, Hug me baby,
Hug me, Hold me baby,
Bay-bee, Hold meeeee."

"Look at that yacht, Andre. Going up the river. Can you see it? Much bigger than your father's. I'll bet it crossed the ocean." Her face brightened like a white saucer.

"I've got tickets for a musical this Saturday night," he said.

"Can't make it."

"I didn't ask you."

"Oh." She smiled warmly and stroked the back of his neck. "I didn't understand."

"Stop that Marsha." He shook his head as if to frighten off a fly. "You're disturbing me. Cut it out." She smiled and continued to stroke his neck. "Do you want us to crash?" he demanded. She stopped and faced forward.

"...Hold me pretty baby.

Hug me pretty baby,

Bay-bee. Bay-bee. Hug meeeeeeeee." The male trio ended the song on a shrill falsetto. Andre snapped off the radio.

"Marsha, I want to talk to you. Seriously. I'm going to pull over."

"You can't park on the highway! Don't get crazy!"

"There." He nodded in the direction of a little inroad.

"It's allowed for repairs."

She shrugged. "You'll get a ticket I'm sure."

He turned in quickly and stopped the car with a jerk. He turned off the ignition and pulled the emergency brake. "We've got repairs to make, you and me.'

"Don't be silly. Everything's just fine, don't you think?"

"Is it? How about this Meyers guy? Is he taking up your time?"

"Not much." She resented this badgering; first Bill and now Andre too. They had no right to pressure her, whatever their motives. Look at the river, slow and majestic in places, swift in others, but flowing at its own pace, its own direction; unhurried by the ships, unmindful.

"Marsha, you know how I feel. If I think you're seeing Meyers or any other guy it upsets me terribly. I can't help it. Forgive me, Marsha, will you forgive me?"

'Yes, of course. Don't I always. You're very sweet Andre." She caressed his face. "I've always thought so and I always will."

"What do you mean by that?" The muscles of his face tightened and he seemed suddenly old. He reminded her of Ross, her ex-husband; the same worried, pleading, plaintive aspect, followed by glum resignation.

147

"Nothing." She laughed. "Nothing at all, silly." Suddenly she thought it time she was a mother; it was this unexpected idea at this inappropriate moment that made her laugh. The strangest thing about ideas; they appeared out of nowhere, yet they belonged...

"It's not funny Marsha. I want to marry you. I've told you a hundred times. We've been waiting--well, that's your idea. But it's foolish. I know you Marsha. Forgive me for being frank, Marsha, but you need a man. You're the kind that needs a man. It would be my pleasure, my joy, I swear it. And it would be right for you, for both of us. I know it. I know what's right for us."

"Do you?" She looked away from him to the trim close cropped lawn and the orderly woods beyond. All men think they understand women, know what they need. They're so sure, in their ignorance. Actually they don't know what's right for themselves. Perhaps driving an automobile like this one gives them confidence. Controlling the power and direction of two tons of steel and glass and rubber with the twist of a smooth wheel, comfortable behind the gleaming chrome and sloping windshield, they might see a woman as a simple thing. The dashboard gadgets were so efficient, the car's operation so effortless; a woman, too, must seem to be a creature to be mastered and driven. But they were not so sure of themselves in the night, standing before you in their nakedness, paunchy and awkward and wanting. Then they seemed like little boys seeking the reassurance of their mothers.

"You're right," she said. "I do need a man."

"You need me." He slipped his arm around her shoulders and kissed her passionately.

"Why don't we go away for a weekend?" she suggested, breaking away. "We never have. We could find out if we're compatible, living together."

"Yes," he said enthusiastically. "Sure. I'll make all the arrangements. Where do you want to go?"

"Anyplace out of the city. Where there's water, a lake or the ocean. Don't make arrangements. Let's just go."

Andre smiled; he seemed contented and confident. "But we have to know where we're going. And what clothes to take. It's better to have a reservation too. Don't' worry about a thing. I'll handle it. How about Montauk? Lots of hotels and motels there; and the ocean. Want to go this weekend?"

"I thought you had theater tickets."

"I don't," he admitted. "But I can get them. I thought you were busy."

"I am. Let's make it next weekend."

"Oh Christ. Who are you busy with this weekend?"

"What difference does it make?" she declared angrily. "Maybe I've got relatives coming in."

He was silent. Then he asked, "do you?"

"Yes," she hissed.

"Bitch," he muttered.

"What did you say?"

"Marsha, do we have an understanding or don't we? At the party you said we were engaged. Then you denied it. Now you want to go away for a weekend. But you're still fighting me. You've got to be square with me. What are you thinking of?"

She sighed. "I told you. We'll go away the weekend after this." Her tone softened. "Be patient, Andre. Trust me."

"I do Marsha. That is, I want to. Whatever you say is okay with me. That's the way our life would be, Marsha, whatever you say. Forgive me if I ask too many questions. I can't help it. You're my rock, Marsha. My foundation. When we're together on Thursday nights.... I depend on you. I build on you. I never felt this way before; that's why I want you so, why I need you. This must be something; don't you believe it?"

She smiled and embraced him, pulling him against her bosom. "Yes," she said. He lay there quietly and she stroked his ear and the back of his neck. His eyes were closed. Marsha relaxed against the seat cushion. They remained that way for several minutes until a police car pulled alongside.

"Hey," the officer shouted, "what's the trouble here?" Andre straightened quickly, adjusting his tie. "Everything's fixed now," he said.

"Get movin'. Get movin'. This is no lovers' lane."

Andre started the engine and they turned back toward the city. The sun was a red ball above the highlands of New Jersey; it sent a bolt of flaming light upon the river, seeming to point toward them.

"You'll come Thursday night, Marsha, like always."

"Yes, I'll come." She sighed. The river was patches of black and blue and white over a barely visible current. The flaming reflection of the sun split the water in two.

"You won't forget Marsha. I'll phone you Wednesday night, so you'll remember."

"I won't forget," she said, suddenly weary, the humidity, dull and oppressive, like a slab of weight upon her.

"It'll be like old times. Thursdays at the Blaine's. We can plan about the weekend then. We'll have a great time. We can plan about the future too. Right Marsha? Our future, right?"

"Yes Andre."

Chapter 18

The carpeted elevator silently swept Sylvia up the aluminum-sheathed skyscraper and softly deposited her before the glass entranceway to Atkins and Holton, "Specialists in Selling." Playfully she swung her tan leather handbag, breaking the invisible electric current that snapped back the doors. Then, helloing the platinum blonde receptionist, she strode onto the spacious office floor, past several glass partitioned cubicles, to her own. After a quick examination of her tidy desk she poked into the mail and message receptacle with the curiosity and excitement of a child seeking Christmas gifts.

Arriving at work usually exhilarated her, especially since A.&H. moved from its overcrowded five rooms near Times Squares to the new Bargey Building on Madison Avenue. She could neither understand nor sympathize with many of her fellow workers, men mostly, who grumbled so in the mornings, mooning about their weekends in the country or at the seashore, their golf games and cocktail parties. They seemed to live in anticipation of sneaking out early Friday afternoons. Sylvia, on the other hand, often found herself unaccountably sad as the week ended and occasionally she lingered alone, except for the cleaning women and the flickering of the setting sun's rays on the rows of vacant chairs and desks; then she felt like the ruler of a deserted kingdom.

Five years ago Josh Holton hired her as his secretary. He was a one-man agency then. (Andrew Atkins, his brother-in-law, invested most of the money for the fledgling firm but he seldom came to the office.) After several weeks on the job she volunteered for copywriting chores and asked her boss to teach her the techniques of advertising. He agreed, after warning that the ad work would have to be in addition to her regular duties and that her $65 weekly salary could not be increased at that time. But Sylvia thrived on work; only dullness and inactivity fatigued her. She labored at home over Mr. Holton's assignments and, in addition, enrolled in a City College evening course: Layout and Copywriting. They did not come easily to her and she was far from the brightest student in her class. But she was determined not to be another 9-to-5 secretary who flocks to public dances and upstate resorts, priming herself with expensive clothes in the hope that some clerk or salesman would marry her.

As Mr. Holton's secretary she learned every aspect of the business: the legal byways, the process of negotiating with clients and other agencies, how to deal with newspapers, wire services, magazines, radio and television. She quickly lost her timidity with the so-called bigwigs in the news, advertising and entertainment media; more slowly, she mastered the basics of advertising copy, publicity releases, design and layout. After eight months Mr. Holton offered her a full-time advertising job.

"I'm truly impressed with your interest and your progress," he had said. "And I need an assistant. So, if you like, I'll hire a new secretary."

She did not have to be asked twice. With a $10 raise, a new desk and a swivel chair, she commenced her advertising career. The firm was growing, largely because of Mr. Holton's indefatigability and persuasiveness and because the country was prosperous and businessmen in post-war America were becoming more conscious of the value of publicity and advertising. New personnel were hired, some bringing business with them, others taking over incoming accounts. Sylvia's responsibilities increased and so did her salary, to $100 a week. But, while newcomers were generally paid more and given bigger opportunities, she continued as Mr. Holton's assistant. Her handicap, she realized, was starting without experience. Others, bouncing from one ad agency to another, had built reputations that were lengthy if not solid.

Subtly, she campaigned for her own account, a chance to show what she could do independently. When the Jeff H. account arrived, Mr. Holton gave her hope. Though he was the direct liaison with the client, she was given a free hand to develop her own ideas. At the opportune moment, if all went well, Mr. Holton promised to give her full authority.

She was clipping an unusual ad from a morning newspaper when Mr. Holton entered her cubicle.

"Morning Sylvia," he said. "I'm seeing the Hanford people at eleven. Anything special I can tell them."

"Yes. I think we'll have that Sunday feature with Intercontinental News."

He pressed his fingertips together, as if in prayer.

"Wonderful. Excellent. Haven't mentioned it yet. Never good to build false hopes. But it'll tie in perfectly with the TV time. Who's your contact up there?"

"Jack Stopple." She swallowed the name.

"Stopple, Stopple, hummmmm…. Never heard of him. Can he swing it himself?"

"The story's been approved by their features department, but the plug could be edited out there."

"Yes, yes." He glanced up at the ceiling and his eyes closed for a moment. "But I can help you on that. Very good. Very good. A nationwide spread…. Hope we don't owe this Stopple much. The budget won't take it. What did you have to promise?"

"Nothing," she said weakly; then she added, with more force, "not a thing."

"Wonderful. Sylvia, that's terrific. A bonus for old man Hanford. Say, have you noticed how flabby he's becoming? I'm tempted to recommend one of his gyms, but I don't trust his sense of humor…. Well, that's encouraging. We don't owe a thing…. Now the Hanford interview on the William Whistler show – that's costing half the national debt to line up."

"But the Jeff H. angle isn't definite," she said. "There could be a last minute change before the story is sent."

"Don't worry." He smiled. "I've got a friend in I.N. features. Tom Nichols. Have I mentioned him to you? He's helped us before. I must write myself a memo to take him to lunch. Don't worry. If you've got tentative approval, we're in. Wonderful. But at this point I'll only suggest the project to Hanford. Light a tiny fire under him."

He started to leave but immediately returned. "Don't think I'm going to grab the credit for this Sylvia. You've done the work and you deserve the rewards. In fact, this may be the moment for you to take over… yes…. Perhaps you can tell Hanford what you've been doing, then I can spring the idea. How does that sound?"

"Fine, Mr. Holton."

"Yes, sir, you're going to get full credit for your work, and the rewards." He parked on the edge of her desk. "Why are we continually maligned as liars, cheats and back-stabbers? We believe in fair play. We're only doing a job, and our job happens to be the most essential task in the nation: persuading people to do what's right for themselves…."

Sylvia recognized the theme of an advertising luncheon speech she had written for him weeks ago. Now she was the audience and had only to look interested and listen.

"…. Competition and cooperation are not mutually exclusive. They can and do operate together. We compete for business; that's free enterprise, our life's blood. Competition sharpens our instruments and strengthens our purpose. But we cooperate to promote our industry. We help our clients compete with their competitors. But we don't try to destroy others; we merely boost our clients. Essentially, we're only giving credit where credit is due. We want to cooperate with the public and the mass media. Yet time and again the very media that depends on advertising for its own existence denounces us.

"The other day a Daily Blade editorial condemned television advertising for frightening the public into the purchase of patent medicines. Don't the editorial writers read their own newspaper? They peddle enough violence to numb any public to what they may view later on TV. But the point is that though the newspapers compete with TV for the advertising dollar they needn't be mortal enemies. Excesses on television are duplicated in another ways in the newspapers. What must be considered is the necessity of a vigorous adverting industry; what must be pondered is the future of our nation if advertising is discredited.

"Politicians decry us. But where would they be without the paid-for and especially the free publicity they get every day in the press, radio and television. The church defames us. Perhaps you read Bishop Green's sermon reprinted in the Gazette. Now I ask you, would he be speaking from the pulpit of such a fine new church if religion itself did not employ the techniques of publicity and advertising. If Bishop Green dared tell the truth, he'd admit that Jesus Christ was the world's first great public relations man. And He sold the message of God damn well!"

The telephone rang on Sylvia's desk. "What?" Mr. Holton asked, as if the ring had been a question. "Oh. Sorry to have kept you Sylvia. You're doing fine. And we're on the same team, yes sir. Answer your phone. I'll be back later."

She lifted the receiver but did not speak until her boss had gone. Jack suggested they lunch together.

"Sure," she said. "It's time I take you on my expense account."

Jack was outside the Madison Avenue Café when she arrived shortly after one o'clock. They kissed lightly and then found a small corner table inside. Sylvia ordered a Manhattan.

"I mentioned the feature to my boss today," she said.

"He was very pleased."

"He should be. But you told him the Jeff H. plug could be edited out?

"Yes." She was about to disclose her boss' connection with Nichols in I.N. features. But she decided it might disturb him. Men often accused women of talking too much, spilling their every thought for public display; perhaps they were right, in general.

"Do you have any misgivings?" she asked, poised on the brink of a new idea.

"No. That's finished. Let the I.N. brass glimpse my name for a change."

"Will it mean a raise, or a promotion?"

He smiled. "No. One story doesn't do that much."

She wanted to tell him that it might mean that much or even more to her career; she wanted to talk about the meeting with Holton this morning and the encouragement he gave her. But again she hesitated, unsure how he would accept this knowledge, fearful that he might resent it, as men so often resented progress in a woman's career.

Instead, she said, "Why don't you write another health story?"

He laughed softly. "This one hasn't gone out yet. Beside, there aren't many things about the field that haven't been said a hundred times before."

"You could write about the growing demand for special foods and vitamin enriched products?" she was moving out of character. She was abandoning the sweet docile acquiescent girl that she had toiled to create especially for him and was returning to the prodding career woman, a person closer to what must be her true self. The success-hungry female was not the prettiest picture to present to a man; it had almost ruined her relationship with Jack earlier. But now she had a new plan.

"Think of all the health fads nowadays, the special diets, the special drinks. You could tie in the anti-cholesterol foods and their relationship to heart disease. Then there are the salt-free and sugar-free products. And almost everybody's counting calories."

"Yes," he mused. "Must be a big industry growing up around these ideas."

"It's a natural follow-up to the exercise story," she said.

"I could help you with it."

"Whoa now." His eyes narrowed and he looked at her with what seemed to be sly amusement. "Does it just so happen that one of your accounts specializes in health products?"

She smiled and sipped her drink. He was eating slowly, relaxed and self-confident, unaware that she had decided to shatter the illusion he probably had of her. It was an appropriate moment, she thought; it had to be done. The I.N. feature was a step up, but more was needed. A momentum had been created that must be pursued. Jack could help again, but she would have to become aggressive again. There were dangers, but she must risk them for the opportunities. Look how the Russians repeatedly turned hot, then cold to advantage: applying strong pressure at one moment, creating a crisis, and then, releasing suddenly, ending the threats and talking only of peace. These tactics prevented the United States from formulating an adequate response; it was impossible to defend against an adversary whose position shifted so radically.

"It does so happen," she said, without looking at Jack but tipping her cocktail glass by its stem so that the liquid slipped to the edge, "that Jumbo Products is starting a health food division. It could tie in easily."

"Sylvia," he said, still a trace of humor in his voice, but tinged with impatience. "I can't promote your clients. What if my bosses found out? What if they suspected payoff?"

"Their only complaint would be that they weren't included."

"Wait a minute," he objected. "The news business isn't completely corrupt."

"I never said it was," she insisted. "What's wrong with mentioning a product or a company in a news story. You wouldn't hesitate if the company were involved in a strike or a law suit, or if the product were injurious in some way? Why is the news always partial to what is evil, and suspicious or disinterested in what is good?"

Jack patted her hand. "The way you put it makes sense. Still, I have the feeling – an intuition – that though the logic may be right, the results would be wrong."

"Now you're going mystical on me," she said. "If we agree on logic then we are agreed. After all, you're intuition may be only a gastric disturbance."

They laughed together. "Sylvia Parker, you know my stomach muscles better than that."

Chapter 19

The annual dinner-dance of the New York Reporters Club was conceived as a family affair. Newsmen from rival organizations and media would socialize in an alcoholic glow while their wives could verify that other reporters were equally housebroken. It was to be an evening of good fellowship, a dress-up affair for the missus, concluding with ensemble hilarity and drunkenness.

But like most good ideas, this one contained flaws. A few reporters, clinging to their rakish traditions, jarred the picnic atmosphere by escorting flashy showgirls. Others, like Jack Stopple, were unmarried and had abandoned the liquid rites. Finally, a crushing drawback was money.

To protect its solvency in hiring a spacious ballroom, an orchestra, and in providing good food and drink, the club fixed a $50 a couple admission. Proceeds, if extant after expenses, went to charity. Thus the affair became a charity ball, hence tax-deductible. But when the tab was added to the cost of transportation, including taxies, a baby sitter, a corsage for the lady, perhaps a new gown or a rented tuxedo, plus the inevitable tips and unforeseen extras, the total frequently topped a working stiff's weekly take-home pay. (A "working stiff" toils for a fixed wage from which his employer thoughtfully deducts federal, state and city taxes, health and life insurance premiums, union dues and assessments, social security, pension plan, and loan company attachments. His expense account, if he has one, is severely limited.)

So, to insure a full house – the Hotel Broadmoor seats 1,200 in the main ballroom and its two balconies – the club invited paying guests. (Now part of American folkways, the paying guest, in less formal affairs, arrives with a gift, usually liquor, to cover his cost to his host, or alternatively, invites him to consume equal quantities at his abode.) The guests: politicians, corporate and labor officials, and their publicity crews, were happy to pay their way. They recognized immediately the benefits of learning the first names Saturday night of those who might fire embarrassing questions at them Monday morning.

But not only selfish motives drew the guests. Except for superficial differences (hand-tailored clothing, fancy suburban homes) and hobbies, such as yachting and high-class call-girls, the guests were indistinguishable from the newsmen. They were all regular guys. The officials and their press agents liked the reporters so much they began buying their tickets. Since the cost could be tax-deducted twice, for charity and as a business expense, the practice spread like atomic fallout. Each year the club invited more guests, who, in turn, invited more reporters to be their guests. Before long, reporters not offered a free ticket stopped attending, for, even if they could afford to, they felt socially inferior to those invited. Soon the club was aware of a dangerously developing situation: the proportion of newsmen was constantly diminishing and the character and intent of the ball was threatened. To correct the imbalance, the ticket committee worked feverishly this year to increase reporter representation. It resulted, for example, in the presence of Jack Stopple, who strolled through the mirrored lobby escorting Sylvia.

She smiled, supremely happy as she steered the flowing skirt of her white gown into the huge ballroom profusely decorated with red and white roses, chrysanthemums, violets, patriotic streamers, and suspended over the stage, the green and gold club emblem. Jack appeared rather stiff and self-conscious but handsome as a movie star in a black tuxedo, which, she suspected, had been rented for the evening. Sylvia liked balls, all big splashy events; the lights and colors and the gay chatter over the sound of muted music exhilarated her. But this ball, she felt, would be especially significant: a chance to mingle with the big names in news and politics and business and publicity, her clients and contacts. She had, in fact, offered to buy the ticket, insisting that Atkins and Holton would pay and knowing the expense would burden Jack. But he had refused.

After greeting several people along the way, they reached their table, excellently located near the dance floor.

"Hi," exclaimed Sylvia, "how nice to see you again." She extended her arm like an artificial limb. It was grasped by Ann Rawley who half-smiled in response and glanced quickly at Jack, seeming to avoid his eyes. Stanley Cowels, in a double-breasted tuxedo, stood up, holding the back of his chair. The others at the table were introduced: the police department's public relations officer and his wife, and Tom Burland, an old time I.N. police reporter, and his wife.

"Didn't expect to find you here," said Jack.

"I'm rejoining civilization," replied Cowels. "Shed my leopard skin. See?" He indicated his tuxedo.

"Quite an improvement," said Jack.

A frown passed quickly over his face. "I'm not sure. Trying to please my lady love." He touched Ann's hand.

"My," cried Sylvia, "what an influence."

"It's entirely his idea," said Ann. "Actually, I prefer his turtle-neck sweater."

"Wonder who's got those?" Burland nodded toward the last two empty seats. Nobody knew. He poured drinks from the bottles of scotch and rye on the table.

Each place was set with a deep dish of cut orange, pineapple and grapefruit slices, topped with a large strawberry. Alongside the silverware was a complimentary pack of cigarettes and at every alternate setting, a flasket of branded perfume. The gifts rested on a 178-page color program which included articles by newsmen and many ad greetings from firms and individuals whose names were often in the news.

The orchestra was playing "society music," a quick undanceable beat that permits poor dancers to rival the more expert, and, when they had finished the ox-tail bouillon that followed the fruit cup, Ann and Cowels, and Sylvia and Jack, went out on the crowded floor.

"I'm enjoying this," said Cowels, "because you're with me. I'd be lost without you, cherie`."

"You're a good dancer," replied Ann, smiling pleasantly. "Surprise, surprise."

A flicker of pain crossed his eyes. "I noticed the way you looked at Jack, or didn't rather. Still care for him?"

"No." She laughed. "He's a nice guy. But you're much more distinguished. Besides, he seems pretty-well occupied."

They danced without speaking; then Cowels said, "you are considering my proposal Ann. I meant it seriously... The boys love you too, I know, and you seem to like them."

"I do, Stan. You have fine sons. So well behaved; just like their papa."

"Okay baby, enough schmaltz."

"I've written to my parents about you, but I didn't mention marriage."

"Scared?"

"No." She drawled out the word. "It would be nice if we could travel there, together, with your boys. A long weekend maybe."

"That does sound good. A bit expensive, but worthwhile."

"Think about it. It was just an idea."

"I will," said Cowels. "I certainly will."

The band launched a samba and they returned to the table, arriving at the same time as Jack and Sylvia. Hardly had they been seated when Mark Larson arrived. He asked Sylvia if the chairs next to her were occupied.

"Must be mine," he added, sitting before she could reply.

"Hello Mark," said Burland. "How are you?" He introduced his wife, who twisted her napkin furiously.

"Stan Cowels! How goes it?" Larson got up and shook his hand.

"Fine, Mark. So you remember old friends. I knew you were better than your reputation."

"Where you been? Hollywood? Bull fights in Spain?"

"Not quite." Cowels grinned sardonically; his upper lip curled slightly. "Plenty of bull in New York. I'm at I.N., on rewrite."

"Yeah, sure," said Larson. To Jack he said, "I've seen you before," and, as if that were sufficient, he turned away to the others.

Two city politicians came over to welcome Larson. "No, can't stay long," he replied. The waiter asked if he wanted the soup course. "Just the meat and potatoes," he snapped. When the politicians left he asked Sylvia to dance. She glanced at Jack, who said, "sure, go ahead."

"Can't resist the samba," said Larson, leaning in Jack's direction and winking. Then he led Sylvia away.

Jack turned to Burland and said, rather loudly, "why don't you tell the story of Jack Pierson's death, the unprinted version, I'll bet the ladies would get a kick out of it."

"No," replied Burland. "It's not for mixed company." He spoke to his wife and Jack tried to locate Sylvia on the dance floor. But there were too many dancers.

"Sylvia Parker. That's the way I caught your name."

Larson held her firmly about the waist as they swayed to the latin rhythm.

"Yes."

"In publicity, aren't you?"

"How did you know?" she asked.

"That's my business: to know things. Don't you see my program?" His narrow lips smiled tightly.

"Sometimes. Viewing TV is one of the duller aspects of my job."

"Thanks. I don't bruise easily." He added, "neither do you."

"You seem to know all about me."

"Not all. But I can tell about people. It's a game I play. Usually I'm right. In your case I'm cheating. I saw you at Ann Rawley's party."

"You remember that." She was truly surprised. "I was walking out."

"I inquired about you. Suspected we'd meet again."

Sylvia was impressed, yet disconcerted; he stared at her continually, his eyes strangely vacant and cold. The rhythm and melody were sensuous and gay, but they danced mechanically and without joy.

"I do see your program," she said suddenly, with forced cheer. "I like the style, though it isn't original."

"Encore. I'm going to like you. You're not tied to that guy are you? I don't see any sparklers."

"No," she replied. "But you're married."

"How did you know? Does it show?"

"It's a game I play," she said, her eyes narrowing.

"I can tell about people." They laughed; the music stopped and they returned to the table.

"Sharp," noted Larson, still chuckling. "Very sharp."

"What's the joke?" asked Jack, his brow creased.

"Secret," replied Larson, "revealed only on channel one."

Sylvia squeezed Jack's hand.

As the grilled filet mignon was being served, a wine steward wheeled over a bottle of champagne packed in an ice bucket. "Compliments of Karl Billings Associates, table 22," he said, "for Mr. Larson."

"Wonderful," exclaimed Larson. "Bring wine glasses for everybody." He excused himself. "Must thank Karl."

He returned in a few minutes. "Nice people, Billings Associates," he told Sylvia. "Who are you with?" When she replied he remarked, "ah yes, I know Josh Holton. Sweet guy."

The champagne went around the table once, barely filling the glasses. Larson ordered another bottle; when it arrived the other men offered to share the expense, but Larson waved them off.

"No no," said Burland, whose eyes were slightly glassy.

"I insist. This bottle's on me."

"I ordered the champagne and I'm paying," said Larson, smiling his tight thin-lipped smile. He reached into the inside pocket of his tuxedo and withdrew a small pearl handled pistol which he laid on the table.

"Any objections," he added.

"Hey, hey, put that thing away," said Burland, standing up suddenly and then slowly sitting down in place.

"What a pretty toy," said Ann. It is a toy, isn't it?"

"Certainly, my dear," said Larson. He pocketed the gun and signaled the wine steward. "Burland, you always were too stubborn," he added, signing the check for the champagne which the steward had presented.

The music began again, diverting those at the table; several couples danced. "He's quite a character," said Jack. "Out of the movies," replied Sylvia. When they returned to the table, coffee was served. Trumpets played a fanfare as the club president walked onto the stage. He thanked everyone for attending and making the event "the most successful in our history." In twenty minutes, he said, entertainment would begin.

When the orchestra started up again, Larson asked Sylvia for "a last dance."

"Listen," he said as they reached the dance floor, "I'm leaving for the Whirlwind Club. A table's reserved for me there. New show opening tonight. Will you come?"

"Sounds fun," replied Sylvia, "but I'm not free tonight."

"I know, I know. Can't you ditch him? Later, say. Do that. I'll be waiting. Ask for my table."

Sylvia did not reply. She knew she should say no, but he had not demanded an answer. He held her close and they twirled into an intricate pattern; then he slowed and whispered, "it won't be released until next week but my program is going coast-to-coast. Don't breathe a word."

Larson said goodbye to those at the table, after returning Sylvia to her seat, and then he left. When he had gone Sylvia inquired about Larson's wife. Cowels said they had been separated for years. Burland poured another round of drinks and the conversation veered to the weather. But Sylvia was silent, thinking.

From a business viewpoint, Larson was a valuable acquaintance. He would soon become more important; he had revealed that to her, knowing she would be challenged. Could he fathom her amid the contradictions she perceived in herself? Of course she did not have to meet him tonight. She could telephone his office or visit another day. But would her reception then be cold and formal? She had never been to the swanky Whirland; it would be a glamorous, glittering night, and she would be up front with a strange unpredictable escort. Here, it was becoming dull. She was disappointed; one could not mingle; she was stuck at the table and with Jack. He was becoming dull, too; a nice guy, handsome, affectionate, but essentially empty, lifeless, contemplative, uncertain, fearful, a young man in a crowd, certainly nobody to sweep her above the mundane. Probably Larson would not either. No use kidding oneself. But Larson was the unknown, the opportunity.

The entertainment was about to begin: singers and dancers and perhaps a comedian; it might last hours. Sylvia wanted to flee. A new path was open and she wanted to follow; the moment was ripe. There was a light, a silly glimmer, wavering, flickering, unreliable, but it existed now, perhaps only for the moment. That was the thrill of life, the beauty; suddenly, when least expected, a new vista was revealed, daring you to explore. But Jack would not understand; that was the crucial difference between them. He would be insulted, believing she preferred another man.

A plan flashed in her mind. She told Jack she was tired and suddenly ill, perhaps from the drinks. Jack suggested he take her home immediately, and he did. At the door she apologized for spoiling his evening, but he said he was perfectly contented, adding that he would telephone in the morning. Fifteen minutes after Jack departed she descended into the street again and hailed a taxi for the Whirlwind Club.

Chapter 20

Jack awoke Sunday morning like a bright pupil, immediately alert and eager. He exercised in Central Park and, following a hot, then cold shower, telephoned Sylvia, hoping she would match his high spirits. Marsha answered; she said her roommate was well, but had returned to bed after breakfast, leaving instructions not to be disturbed. The day passed quickly and the next, also his day off, was uneventful. He telephoned Sylvia's office but she was out. In the evening Bill called, and after awhile asked how he had enjoyed opening night at the Whirlwind Club.

Jack said he was mistaken. "I was at the Reporters Club dance with Sylvia."

"I knew you were together Saturday night," said Bill.

"Didn't you go to the nightclub afterward?"

"Can't afford to on the stocks you've recommended."

"No kidding. Sylvia's picture is in the Blade today, taken Saturday night at the Whirlwind.

"Must be a twin," suggested Jack.

"But her name was printed, too, on the society page."

"Well, that's the way these publicity gals operate, always getting their names in the news."

"Just the same, look at today's Blade. It's her, I'm sure."

"Okay detective Meyers."

Jack's curiosity aroused, he was tempted to run downstairs and buy the newspaper. Instead, he telephoned Sylvia to share the joke.

"... then Bill asked me how I enjoyed the Whirlwind."

"I want to talk to you about that," she said. "Will you come over?"

Jack went to two newsstands to find a copy of the morning newspaper, He wanted to see the photograph before meeting Sylvia. It was a group picture with Sylvia seated next to a scowling Mark Larson.

"I felt better after you left, and decided to go," she explained in her apartment. "Mark had invited me earlier, at the ball."

"Is it Mark already?"

She shrugged. "He doesn't change things between us."

"Of course not," agreed Jack. After a pause he added, "why didn't you say he had invited you?"

"I didn't think it important. Really didn't expect to go."

Jack told himself to forget the incident. "I'd like to meet you Friday after work," he said. "We could ...."

"Have you thought about another health feature?" she interrupted. "I'm doing a piece on a new carrot juice to be called 'Whammo.' Ever drink carrot juice?"

"Once," he said, smiling. "In a health bar. Tasted awful."

"Trick is to add artificial flavoring," said Sylvia.

"Jumbo products will market it this month." She removed several papers from a folder. "Want to see a feature idea I've been working on?"

"Not tonight, Syl. I... I think I ought to wait a bit on any new features. But about Friday night I ...."

"I'm busy Friday," she broke in.

"With Mark?"

"Let's make it Thursday, she suggested, taking his arm.

"I'll come to your place. All right?"

"You didn't answer my question."

"Don't press me Jack," she flared. "We've never been that way and we're not going to start now."

"I didn't mean to annoy you," he began and then, dissatisfied with his response and suddenly angry, he said, "I have some rights don't I?"

"No," she said, standing tense, the papers crumpling slightly in her hand. After a moment's electric silence she smiled and leaned her head against his shoulder. "I'll come Thursday, about seven." She held up her face for him to kiss.

Sylvia came promptly Thursday evening, carrying a bottle of champagne and a white box containing Hungarian pastry. "Tonight we celebrate," she exclaimed. "You're going to drink with me, too, even if I have to force it down your gullet." She tossed her jacket on the bed. "Guess?" she demanded, her eyes glistening. "I've got the Jeff H. account."

"Thought you had it already," said Jack, turning over the steak in the broiler.

"This means full charge. I'm account executive!" She threw her arms around his back and hugged him.

"Easy now." He reached for a tin of carrots and peas.

"Well, that's great, congratulations." He kissed her on the cheek.

"What's more I get a $15 raise and my own secretary assistant," she cried.

"Want a salad tonight? I've got lettuce and tomatoes."

"Don't you realize what this means?" She hung on to him. "Can't you see my penthouse coming closer?"

"Yes. Will you invite me for dinner?"

"Jack," she spoke his name as if to admonish him. "Let me finish here. Out. Out of the kitchen!" She unfastened his apron from behind. After dinner they left the dishes piled in the sink.

"Good stuff," said Jack, sipping the champagne. "You're liable to overturn my whole health program with this." He raised his glass and clinked hers. "You never told me about the Whirlwind show."

"Big and brassy," she said. "Lots of girls in panties. I was sorry you weren't there."

"I'll bet you were."

"I was," she insisted. "Oh darling, I feel so marvelous tonight. Just think. Me. An account exec at 26, with my own secretary!" she gulped her drink and flung herself into his arms, burying her head on his chest, curling like a cat. He carried her to the bed and they tumbled onto it. Lazily he reached for the lamp switch.

Afterward he drove her home, double parking outside her apartment house.

"Are you seeing Larson tomorrow night?"

"Don't be jealous Jack. He means nothing to me."

"Can't help it. I love you Sylvia." He leaned forward to kiss her but she backed away.

"Jack…." She avoided his eyes. "I don't want you to love me. I don't want you to care for me too much."

"Oh, that's funny." Laughter rattled in his throat.

"I'm not ready to get serious, with anyone."

"I am," he declared firmly. He grasped her shoulders and turned her to face him. "I've written to my parents about you, about us. They've been after me for years to get married. I said I might have news for them soon."

"Stop," she said weakly, pressing her fingers to his lips. "You had no right to do that. We never spoke about it."

"I didn't think we had to. Sylvia, don't you see us together, always?"

Even in the dimness in the car he could see the anguish in her eyes. "Where? Up in my dream penthouse, off on the moon or in a tiny flat where we'd be at each other's throats in no time? Jack,

170

I'm just beginning to live. I can't get tied down now. I thought you understood. We're friends; Jack, we're lovers, but … well, isn't that enough?"

His sweaty hand pulled fuzz off the grimy seat cushion.

"Has Larson turned your head already?"

"Of course not. But that's just the point. If I choose to see Mark or anybody else I don't want to apologize to you or anybody for it."

"Sylvia, we need each other. Don't you realize it?"

"I do need you, she said, tears in her voice. "I love you too, but… I can't explain. Only let's not become possessive and demanding. We've never been that way."

"Sylvia I love you. I want you to be my wife….."

"No, stop, no. I must go…." She was crying as she opened the car door and ran into the house.

Thereafter, she seemed to avoid him. Her new job meant added responsibilities, she said, and less free time. When they did meet they often argued about trivial matters; she became irritable quickly and seemed to have developed a temper.

To his annoyance she pestered him about writing a new health feature. When he stalled she declared he had no ambition. But when he said he would do it for her sake she suddenly cooled to the idea. Jack suspected Larson was pursuing her; Larson, the smart-aleck, the know-it-all, the glamor boy, the TV personality; he was to blame for their rift. Jack began tuning his television program regularly, trying to fathom the man from what he said and the way he said it. He was slick, no doubt, but phony. Surely she could see through his glossy veneer.

One night Larson's cameras "visited" a Jeff H. gym, where he interviewed a Hollywood actor.

"I wouldn't miss a day of exercise," concluded the actor, lowering what appeared to be an extraordinarily heavy barbell.

"And that's a star's tip to you," said Larson. "Good health, America, and goodnight."

Jack flipped off the TV set. "Why that son-of-a-bitch," he exclaimed aloud. "What a God-damned plug." He wondered if it were as obvious to the television audience.

When Jack questioned her about Larson she said their relationship was limited to business. But she angered at his questions, and, consequently or not, she saw Jack less. Still they did not break off and once a week or sometimes every other week she would come to his place. Then, in the quiet of his apartment, each a bit tense yet making an effort to avoid a conflict, they would eventually kiss and end in bed.

"You've really got no gripe," commented Bill, after Jack had described their altered relations. "Now with Marsha I've got a headache. Can't make head or tail of her. And that's no pun." He said that since their double date she had slept with him only once again, suddenly, as if it in a whim.

"But usually she won't let me touch her," he said.

"Sometimes she won't even kiss me goodnight!"

He continued eagerly:

"She's a terrific lay. Really great. She knows things, like a whore. Sometimes I think if we stayed in her bed all our lives I'd always love her. Until I got a heart attack. But when we're not in bed we don't get along. We seem to hate each other. I can't figure it; really, it drives me batty."

The following afternoon there was a message from Sylvia canceling their evening date. Jack telephoned her office but could not reach her. On the chance she would still come he waited in his apartment that night. But she did not. He telephoned again the next day but her secretary said she was out. Marsha conveyed the same message. He left his name always, but she did not return his calls. Finally he went to her apartment. Marsha opened the door.

"She's not here," she said immediately.

"Aren't you going to let me in?"

"You didn't come to see me," she said, smiling slightly, but continuing to stand in the doorway.

"Sure I did. Let me in."

"Don't make a scene," she said, and shut the door.

He swore furiously on the way home, slamming his door and then beginning to pace the floor. "If she wants to break off, why the hell doesn't she say so." He punched his fist into his opposite palm. "Or am I too God-damned thick to get the message?" He flung his clothes on the chair and tried to go to sleep, but he could not. "What went wrong?" he demanded of himself. Perhaps Larson was to blame; but he did not explain away everything. Larson was too easy an answer. What about Sylvia? And himself? Had he failed somewhere? Where? How? He tossed about most of the night, arguing aloud occasionally, thinking to himself, dreaming fitfully.

The next evening, Larson's TV show had a new sponsor: Jumbo Products, and a carrot juice called, "Whammo." Larson read the commercial:

"A healthful diet makes for a healthful life. For an invigorating life, drink Whammo. For sound, peaceful sleep, drink Whammo. For the extra step that puts you ahead, drink Whammo. To be a success, drink a successful combination of nature's knowledge. Drink Whammo. It tastes soooooooooooo good."

Impulsively, Jack telephoned Sylvia's apartment; he was startled when she responded immediately.

"I've been calling you for a week," he said.

"I've been terribly busy, Jack. How are you?"

"Lousy. Just saw Larson's Jumbo Products commercial."

"Wasn't it good!"

"Made me nauseous. I hope you didn't write it."

"I'm sorry you've soured on health foods."

"I haven't soured on health foods. I think carrots are great. They've done wonders for rabbits and I'm sure Whammo is just what I need to put me to sleep and invigorate me at the same time."

"Why must you always tear everything apart?" Her question was a cry.

"I'm sorry," he said. "Let's not argue over the phone. Why don't we meet somewhere? I'll come right over."

"No, don't. This may be best, Jack. I'm sorry, but I can't see you anymore, not for dates."

"Why not?"

"For one thing, I'm seeing Mark."

"You mean you're sleeping with him."

"You've no right to insult me. You didn't complain when we were together."

Jack paused; then he entreated, "but Larson's a hoax."

"Not anymore than you. He's sincere in what he is and he doesn't fool himself or me."

"What about us, Syl? Wasn't that worth holding on to?"

"I thought so. I tried. Perhaps you didn't realize it, but I tried. I gave you all I could, but you're not satisfied. I do care for you Jack; that's why I know we've got to call it quits."

"Fine feminine logic! What's happening in the world?? Is it wrong to care?"

"You don't care for me. If you did you'd understand. You want a puppet to play with, someone to jump when you raise a finger. That's not for me. I'm sorry Jack. I hope we can remain friends."

"Were we ever?"

She clicked off.

Chapter 21

The next morning Jack received a telephone call from I.N.'s feature department. "Still want to see your story?" he was asked. He said yes and went up to the 12th floor.

"My name's Nichols." The bulky bespectacled man rose behind his desk; his handshake was firm, belying the flab of his jowls. "Sorry for the delay. The art department held us up. This is the first time I've seen your work. Quite good. We're planning to move it for Sunday release."

"Fine," said Jack. "Have you made any changes?"

"Only minor ones. Let me show you." He opened a thick folder which apparently was crammed with feature materials and handed Jack's to him. It was the same copy he had submitted; a few sentences had been chopped and others edited slightly; one paragraph had been split, but basically it was unchanged. He came to a section toward the end that began:

"The burgeoning interest in health has boomed new commercial enterprises. The Jeff H. Gyms, for example, sprouted from a small exercise room in midtown Manhattan to a national corporation with modern gymnasiums coast to coast. There, in spotless air-conditioned salons under scientifically controlled ultra-violet lighting, thousands learn the fundamentals of body building to the muted strains of recorded music."

Pointing, Jack said, "I think we ought to drop this paragraph."

"Take a look at the dandy cartoons we're sending out with the story," said Nichols. He removed two drawings from another folder; one showed a fat woman struggling to perform deep-knee bends, the other a skinny man hoisting a huge dumbbell.

"I suppose they lighten the piece," noted Jack.

"Oh considerably. Well then, everything is in order."

"This graph mentioning the Jeff H. Gyms," said Jack, "we'd better eliminate it."

"Let me read it again." Nichols yanked off his eyeglasses and perused the copy slowly. "Hmmmmmmm," he murmured. "What's wrong?"

"Don't you think it gives, well, a boost to the Jeff H. outfit?"

"Hmmmmmm." Nichols seemed to reread the passage.

"Nooooo," he drawled.

"Other commercial gyms might say we were favoring this one," said Jack, rubbing his palms against the sides of his trousers.

Nichols pulled a tobacco pouch from one of his desk drawers and pushed his pipe into the loose strands of brown and yellow.

"The Jeff H. Gyms are the largest in the country," he said, flickering open a lighter. "Everything you say is true, isn't it?"

"Yes it's true. But I think it might be misconstrued as publicity. We ought to drop it – to play safe."

Nichols drew in on his pipe several times; then he rubbed his eyes gently. "I don't understand you Stopple. You wrote the story. You put this, ah, paragraph in. We've made the changes we felt necessary. The art work is set. I don't' see why you're complaining?"

"I'm not complaining. Not at all!" Jack inched to the edge of his chair. "I appreciate the work you've done up here. But since I initiated the story I should have something to say about it."

"Naturally, but...." Nichols puffed at his pipe and swung his swivel chair around to face him. "Why did you write the story? You haven't done features for us before."

"The idea just came to me... and I dashed it off. But that isn't the point. I'm pleased with your treatment. It's only this insignificant graph I want cut."

Nichols face hardened, his cheeks firmed like freezing gelatin. "There is a point here Stopple. I.N. strictly forbids publicity. A reporter was fired on the west coast, you probably know, for plugging some racetrack. In features we're very careful about these things."

"Exactly my idea," urged Jack, hardly able to contain himself. "I want to make sure there's no thought of that."

Nichols sighed. "Jack, as I see it, the story reads fine as is. The Jeff H. organization fits logically. There's no question in my mind about that. There's no harm in naming a company or a product. We do it all the time. As long as the intent is honest and above-board, the intent, do you understand?..."

Jack felt his words implied more than they stated, but he did not comprehend Nichols' meaning nor his stubborn refusal on this point.

"...If the intent was dishonest," Nichols continued, his eyes narrowed, seeking out Jack's. "If we believe a feature was written expressly for the purpose of publicizing something..."

He paused again, as if to let the import sink in to his listener. Then he shrugged. "But that's where our judgment comes in." he smiled broadly.

"I don't' understand why this paragraph makes such a difference," said Jack resignedly.

Nichols came slowly around his desk and placed his arm around Jack's shoulders in a fatherly manner. "Leave it to me," he said. "The article's fine. It will get good play across the country, with your byline, of course."

Jack smiled weakly. To argue further appeared pointless and perhaps even dangerous. He had offered to drop the publicity, so there could be no question of his being implicated in any wrong-doing. His motive in this matter, he admitted, was revenge against Sylvia, a rather petty desire. Now he could accept his long-sought byline with a clear conscience.

His arm still over Jack's shoulders, Nichols propelled him toward the exit chatting casual words of encouragement. But Jack was not listening particularly. Strangely, he was reminded of a moment many years ago that returned as if it were happening now. The muffled noise of the teletype machines blended into screaming cheers from the gymnasium of Oakland High School as Sommerset High's basketball team tied the score 68-all with only a minute or two left to play in the season's finale. Jack, active most of the game, felt maddeningly frustrated sitting on the bench in the closing minutes. He rushed to the coach's side and begged to be put in again.

"I can do it, coach, honest, I feel I can do it," he had said.

"Leave the running of the game to me," the coach shouted back curtly. Then, perhaps seeing the hurt in Jack's eyes as he went back to the bench he had recalled him with a flick of his hand. The coach put his arm around his shoulders. "How do you feel?"

"Fine sir," replied Jack.

Then, still clutching his sweaty shoulders, the coach quickly outlined what he wanted the team to execute.

"Have you got it?" the coach yelled into his ear as students in the grandstand behind them screamed. Jack nodded vigorously to reinforce his reply.

"Go to it then," the coach said, sending him onto the floorboards with a smack on his rump.

It had been a ragged game, as season ending traditional rivalries usually were. Oakland, with a flawless record, should have trampled the lowly ranked Sommerset squad. But spirit had counted for more than form and the score seesawed back and forth.

The Oakland coach called for a screen play that Oakland had employed successfully before against a zone defense such as Sommerset's. The team had practiced it often, for it was as difficult as it was effective. Success depended entirely on split-second teamwork and the correct positioning of every member of the squad.

The referee sounded his whistle for time out and Jack drew his tired and sweaty teammates together. "The coach wants number 11, the screen play," he said. "Remember it?"

The others nodded. "Who takes the shot?" asked Petersen, the tall lanky center. "The coach said me," noted Jack. "Any questions?" There were none; they joined hands in the center of the huddle and after a second's silence came out with a shout that spurred the grandstand to a roar.

It was Oakland's ball. Jack passed the leather sphere from the outside to Williams, his fellow guard, who dribbled into the Sommerset court as Oakland's forwards and center raced downcourt into the Sommerset zone defense. Williams passed back to Jack and one of the Sommerset forwards lunged for the ball, barely missing an interception.

The action had taken the forward out of position, leaving Jack unguarded for a moment. Seeing his opportunity, Jack made for the basket, and lifted an easy lay up shot against the backboard. The ball swished through the net: 70 to 68. The grandstand was a confusion of cheers and yells and screams and applause. Only seconds were left; a Sommerset guard passed the ball out; there was a long heave at the Oakland basket as the whistle blew to end the game. Before the ball fell short onto the court the students had burst the barrier, throwing books and hats and papers into the air. Jack was lifted on the shoulders of two cheerleaders. He saw the coach wave happily at him and then turn to go to the locker room with the rest of the squad. Jack tried to get off the shoulders of the cheerleaders to join the team but the crowd was too thick around him. The more he tried to descend the more the students cheered him. Finally, he relaxed and simply waved as he was carried in a triumphant circle around the gymnasium. The band struck up, "For He's A Jolly Good Fellow." He felt both silly and happy amid the hysteria.

Back in the City News department, the black turtle neck sweater of Stanley Cowels recalled Jack's black high school letterman's sweater with a big gold "O" in front and the basketball and track symbols of which he had been so proud.

"Hello sport," said Cowels. "Features like your stuff?"

"Yes," replied Jack, absentmindedly. "A byline story, my first byline in nine years with I.N."

"Congratulations," said Cowels. "You're on your way." He was smiling grimly; the corners of his mouth locked, turning his expression into a wry grimace. He held out his hand and they clasped firmly. Jack saw him now changed from the man he had known. He was straighter, somehow, more solidly built than he had been aware of previously. His hooked prominent nose was daring, rather than awkward, and he noticed, perhaps for the first time, the stubborn cut of his chin. As he held Jack's hand their eyes met. Then Jack's glance slipped to Cowel's black sweater; it had been patched at the elbows but the cloth seemed sturdy and of one piece.

"Be right back," said Jack, breaking away.

"Don't be hasty," Cowels called after him.

Instead of waiting for the elevator Jack ran upstairs to the features department.

Chapter 22

Two tall blue-uniformed ushers flung open the theater exits. A moment later, the patrons, including Bill and Marsha, trickled out of the refrigerated darkness where they had attended the three hour and forty-seven minute reserved-seat production of "They Conquered the West" to be enveloped by the sticky neon-lit night. Ignoring the news hawkers cry of "New Crisis in Asia," they entered an air-conditioned café nearby and ordered coffee and waffles.

"I've got a miserable headache," said Bill, rubbing his temples. "They've no right to make such goddamn long films. Everytime I'm in a movie more than two hours I get dizzy. I should know better than to go."

"Oh I'm sorry," drawled Marsha, reaching across the table and patting his hand. "you can't concentrate long. I thought it was marvelous. All those Indians and killings. Only one thing wrong: with so many Indians and only a handful of Americans, the Indians should have won."

"We had the atomic bomb."

"Bill Meyers, can't you ever be serious?"

"Baby doll I've been trying to be serious with you for... how long have we known each other?... six or seven weeks now, but you...." Bill stopped as the waitress brought their order. She was a slim pretty girl with close-cropped dark hair; Bill perceived what must be a girdle beneath her thin uniform and he imagined her without clothes. The waitress apparently noticed his intense appraisal; she tossed her head like a filly as she left. Bill smeared two pats of butter over his waffles.

"Look Marsha, I don't like being treated like one of your fifth-graders."

"What are you grumbling about now?"

"You know damn well you're giving me a run-around.

I'm a patient guy, but there's just so much hand-holding and Indian movies I can take."

"Do you want to break up?" She forked a slice of waffle into her mouth.

"That's not what I'm driving at."

She patted a corner of her mouth with a napkin to remove a smear of syrup. "Jack and Sylvia broke up," she noted.

"I know. I thought they were doing fine."

"They were. But now she's got Mark Larson."

"Big deal. And how long will he last?"

Never can tell. Anyway, Sylvia gets restless."

"Like you?"

"I'm not the restless type," she replied, accepting the cigarette he had offered. They lit up and sipped their coffee.

"Marsha, you've got to come to my place. Tonight. And no more fooling around once we get there either." He took a quick drag on his cigarette. "I'm frustrated as hell. I can't take it, really. Some nights I need pills to sleep."

"If you want to break up, it's okay with me," she said flatly, fluffing the curl in her hair.

He was incredulous. "You want to?"

"Maybe it's time."

"I thought you wanted to marry me?"

"That was a possibility."

"A possibility!"

"Well you don't, do you?"

"I didn't commit myself," he said cautiously.

"No, of course not," she said curtly, her face becoming slightly mottled. "You just want to play around and sleep with me and talk and talk and talk and then one day you won't call anymore and I'm just supposed to forget everything and be a good sport. I know the routine."

Bill smiled patronizingly. "That's not fair," he protested graciously. "I said before, I love you."

"Andre Blaine loves me," she retorted hotly. "I seldom sleep with him, but still he loves me and he wants to marry me. Maybe I will marry him. He needs me, he understands me; at least he tries to understand me. But with us, as you say, it's a problem. So, when the show's over the only thing to do is quit the theater."

"Well Goddamn," he said softly but with feeling. "A four-hour stupid movie, a splitting headache and now this!" His voice became shriller as he spoke.

"Don't scream," she whispered.

"Why shouldn't I? It would be a hell-of-a-lot more realistic than the noises we've heard for the past five hours."

"Four hours," she corrected, her face relaxing a bit. "We should talk quietly, like adults."

"At last you want to be an adult."

"Bill Meyers, stop insulting me. I don't see why two persons can't split up without a fuss."

"Baby, you knock me out. If you want to throw me over for stuffy Andre Blaine, if you think he's a bigger bargain than …I.…" He did not complete his thought. Midway she patted the lipstick on her mouth. Now she rose.

"Wait a minute," he said, grasping her arm. "Sit down."

They posed that way for a moment, glaring at each other like stars in a silent film, cold hard currents between them. Then he released her arm and relaxed in his chair, expecting her to be seated again, or perhaps head for the ladies room. Instead, she turned on her heel, military fashion, and made for the exit.

Before she reached the revolving door, he called out, "Marsha." But she did not look back. He sat again, watching her disappear through the spinning panels. He was aware suddenly of eyes staring at him around the café and the sound of suppressed laughter behind him. His forefinger tapped the table of its own accord; he dragged at his cigarette and then crushed it in the coffee cup. He was about to go through the revolving door when the cashier demanded the check; he returned to the table to fetch it. More laughter jangled in his ears as he departed, finally.

His heart was pounding, his muscles taut as if he were in danger and had to battle. Marsha was nowhere in sight. He strode along Fifth Avenue into Central Park. The sight of a couple embracing on a bench quickened his pace along the darkened path. Soon he found himself passing the outer cages of the zoo. A quarter moon and the dim electric lamps cast an eerie glow upon the iron bars. Inside the cages, the animals were still, dark shadows. It was like coming to a small silent village late at night when the shutters were drawn and the inhabitants asleep.

He passed the seal pond, its dark waters streaked with silvery light, and halted before the cage of the Siamese tiger. The huge triangular head of the animal reclined on its paws. But suddenly there was a stir and two luminous eyes flashed like beams through the bars.

"You see me, huh, tiger? "Bill gripped the iron railing separating the public area from the bars of the cage. "It was I who captured you in the jungle. Me. I tied your legs and muzzled your mouth and threw you in there."

Bill leaned over the rail and as he spoke the tiger inclined his body, as if he were truly listening. "You're not a wild king anymore; you're a stupid house pet. They've made a goldfish out of you and you take it. Why don't you rise up, tear at the bars, gnash your teeth? Why don't you do something? Roar, Goddamn you, why don't you ROAR!"

His strident voice echoed against the steel gray cage, seeming to bounce off the walls across the expanse of the zoo. The tiger stared but did not stir. It seemed to be looking through Bill, beyond him, out into the silence and the dimness, past the limits of the zoo and the park and the city, far, far into the depths of the night. Bill remained there as if hypnotized by the dark luminous eyes emitting darts of white light. Perhaps several minutes passed. Then the tiger rose to its feet, the legs firming like rubber into steel; its head lifted slightly toward the moon so that its long whiskers reflected the eternal white light; then the tiger opened its huge mouth wide, extending its immense jaws to what must be the animal's limits so that the strong white teeth and particularly the sharp pointed fangs at the sides of his mouth glowed against the shadow that was his body; and then soundlessly, with a flick of a reptile-like tongue, the tiger yawned.

Bill looked about to determine if his shouts had attracted anyone, but the zoo seemed deserted of humans. He started toward the streets, walking briskly; then he broke into a run.

Jack wandered toward the river, trodding the pavement that seemed almost moist along the dark side streets to Columbus Avenue and Amsterdam Avenue and Broadway and beyond. He had gone to bed early, weary from the day's work and the thoughts crowding his mind and the emotions churning the events of the past weeks into a buttery chaos in his heart. But he had not reckoned with the sun, which, though long over the horizon, still made itself felt in his room. The sun had beat on the tar roof of his brownstone for fourteen hours and now, at night, the heat stored in the roof continued to filter through the thin ceiling into his top-floor flat. He lay on his narrow bed naked, sweating the sheets damp. Finally, he tossed on a tee shirt and his khaki trousers and went out; he did not think where he was going, only that he must escape his airless flat, if only for the night.

Sitting on the stoops of the brownstones, on wooden folding chairs, on the sidewalk, heat and humidity had driven men in their undershirts, women in slips and flimsy housedresses, some holding infants asleep in their arms. Children playing in the streets, black yellow white brown, running together in the gutters, oblivious to the warm tar underneath and the mugginess, running as if it were noon instead of nighttime, as if the sticky fly-ash in the air were rose petals.

He was not alone tonight as he wandered toward the river; he seemed part of a pilgrimage, unorganized, sporadic yet vaguely felt, an unconscious mass movement of many peoples and many languages toward the Hudson river. They came in ones and twos and threes, whole families carrying blankets and transistor radios and bottles of wine along the littered side streets that all led to the river. From the height along Riverside Drive he could see them lying together on the grassy lawn alongside the water, shadows bundled together that must be couples, children running along the paths, jumping on the benches, all outlined by the dim glow of the quarter moon.

The scene recalled the flight of the Hebrews from their Egyptian oppressors and the gathering by the Red Sea for a Moses to make the waters part and lead them to safety. He heard the plucking of a guitar and felt a cooling mist off the Hudson that had drifted over the maples and oaks and elms along the banks and would fight a losing battle inland.

Immediately behind him was the monstrous shadow of the 20-story apartment house where Sylvia lived. He had not come there consciously; perhaps his feet had acquired the habit. How often had he come in laughter and hope; was it only habit now, spurred by the will and the yearning? He sat on the curb and idly counted up the fourteen stories to her windows; the lights were on. He thought of going up; perhaps if he saw her he could patch up their love. It was not over with him, nor could he believe she had plucked him out of her system so quickly either. The road tar slid slightly under his foot; it was too hot to think.

And then it happened: Larson came out of the building alone. There was no mistaking his lean body, his peculiar walk, stiff and jerky, as if his spine were unhinged like a puppet on a string. Instinctively Jack sprang off the curb like a hound who has spotted the fox. He had no plan except to pursue; Larson walked off the Drive and down a sidestreet toward Broadway. With long purposeful strides Jack came up behind him mid-way in the street.

"Wait Larson."

He half-turned and paused, obviously startled at being summoned in the dark. "Huh. What do you want? Is that you Stopple?" He began walking again.

"Yes. I want to talk to you."

Larson tilted his head sideward, his straight longish nose reflecting dimly in the dull street lamp. But he did not stop. "I'm in a hurry. Make it another time. In my office. Or call me for lunch."

"Make it now." The authority of his own voice surprised Jack. He had no idea what he would say, but neither did he want to be ignored. He grabbed Larson's arm as it swung and twisted it back, forcing him to halt.

"I trust you're not going to be silly. If you want to talk, talk. We don't have to stoop to juvenile delinquency."

"Maybe they're more civilized than we are." Jack tightened his grip. He could beat him now, knock him to the ground and order him "away from my girl." That was the way of the rough teenagers or the old-fashioned "westerns." He could kill him with his bare hands.

"Well, what do you want Stopple? Let's go to the corner bar and have a drink."

A trickle of sweat started down his forehead into the socket of his eye. Larson was frightened. The manufactured television personality, a real enough power in a make-believe world of advertising and publicity, now bowed to blood and muscle.

"Listen Stopple, I can't stand here all night. Let go of my arm; the circulation's stopping. What's eating you? Sylvia Parker? Why bother me? She's got her own mind. I don't control her."

"You're promoting her clients on TV."

"So what? That's show biz. You've been around. If you've been short-changed it's by her not me. Now be reasonable and let go of my arm. Must have a hellova black-n-blue mark already. We don't want a street brawl; wouldn't look good in the papers, for either of us. She got me a new sponsor. That shouldn't disturb you."

"I love her."

"Well have her. Sure. I'm not in your way. Go ahead, if she wants you."

"You're blinding her with bright lights and bubbly illusions." He was bordering on nonsense, Jack realized. He didn't want to debate; he wanted to hit him.

"Look Stopple, if she craves action she's going to get it, if not with me then with somebody else. Wise up. I'm not the villain in the play. This is a modern story: no heroes and no villains, just characters. See? Now be a pal and loosen that powerful grip of yours...."

Jack released him.

"Thanks buddy. You are a strong boy. Sylvia told me you were a weightlifting nut. But you shouldn't pinch people on dark streets. You can get killed that way you stupid son-of-a-bitch."

The curse whipped like a lash. Jack started for Larson who this time retreated adroitly and pulled a pearl handled gun from his inside pocket.

"If you've been drinking Whammo regularly you can see even in this dimness that I'm holding a .32 automatic. It's fully loaded and I assure you I wouldn't hesitate using it. The notoriety might be just what I need to crack Hollywood."

Jack stepped backward against the hub of a parked car.

"And don't run either," Larson continued, waving the snub nosed instrument as he shifted on his feet. "Just because my little friend cuts the influence of your bulging biceps is no reason to flee, is it? Now get this straight. I didn't steal your steady lay; you lost it with your antiquated mentality. I don't love your Sylvia and she doesn't love me. So we hit it off fine, and that goes for the bedroom, too. Easy Jackie,.. this thing might dent your heart muscle. I'm concerned for your education Jackie, which obviously is out of tune with our world. Sylvia Parker knows what she wants and I know what I want. So we don't fool ourselves. That's why we get along, and TV and bright lights and that other crap in your pretty head has nothing to do with it."

Larson stepped closer to him, keeping the gun always between them. "If you've got excess energy, try a punching bag. If you want to beat up somebody you can start with your Sylvia. But not me! I'd put a slug in you now if I was sure some jerk wasn't watching from a window, itching to testify that I killed in cold blood...."

A slow smile started on his thin lips and rather deliberately he moved away from Jack. But he continued talking.

"You said you love her. Interesting. Want to prove it? Here's your chance. Come and get me, right now. Risk your life for her. That's an old-fashioned measure of love, isn't it? I say Sylvia Parker is a silly slut, like most dames in this town. And you, Jackie boy, don't love her anymore than you love me. Your feeling for her penetrates six inches, Jackie, or is it more?"

Larson laughed. "Well, what are you waiting for?" he taunted. "Maybe I've got a toy in my hand, huh? Or maybe I'll miss you in the dark and then you can wipe the gutter with me. What's your love made of? Anger? Wounded pride? I say that Sylvia Parker doesn't care for you or me or anybody but her own wayward ass. She's the new woman, the liberated woman. Want to defend her?"

Jack waited, his hands dripping sweat, his body tense and aching. Larson had baited a trap and dared him to fall in. His whole being yearned to act, to smash him even at the risk presented. But he waited; Larson was telling him something, too. Larson was humiliating him, yes, but was he also being a friend, or as near to a friend as his cynicism would allow? Man has been suckered into battle since time began. Suckered or forced. But Larson gave him a choice.

"Put the gun away," said Jack hoarsely.

Larson laughed. "Why? So you can drag me back to the stone age? Don't think of this as a weapon. This is a great emancipator. It makes you respect my physical weakness."

Surely some things must be worth fighting for, risking for, even dying for. But would this battle, even if he won, change anything? Or would Sylvia laugh and think him a fool? He had humiliated Larson and now the tables were turned. Should he try to turn them again, only to have Larson try again another time, and so on and on in the idiotic way of the world.

"I'm not coming Larson. You win."

"That's smart. Stay alive. And forget about revenge. I've got friends with muscles too." He started away, replacing the pistol in his jacket pocket, glancing over his shoulder as he went, apparently to make certain Jack did not follow.

Perhaps Larson was right. And Sylvia too. If life were only motion it made sense to keep moving: change partners, change attitudes, but always keep moving. Yet, as much as they moved they were linked together, somehow, in a great rubbery plastic that twisted and stretched but never allowed anyone outside the invisible boundary.

Jack strolled back to the corner. He observed Sylvia's apartment lights still on and decided to go up. Surely Larson's were not the final words.

Sylvia opened the door; she was dressed in a bathrobe and slippers. "Oh," she exclaimed, as if she had expected someone else.

"Let me in," he said.

"Yes," she replied. But she hesitated a moment at the door; then she opened it for him. "I was going to bed." She said stiffly. "You'll have to excuse my appearance."

"Oh come off it. We know each other better than that."

"Of course." But still she seemed tense and formal.

"I met Mr. Mark Larson downstairs. We had a friendly chat."

"Did you? Did you really?" her face brightened. "I'm glad. He's a nice guy, Jack, when you get to know him."

Jack smiled grimly. "He had pleasant things to say about you too."

"Did he? That is flattering. Have you come to an understanding? Is everything all settled? It would be nice if we could all be friends. That would be best. I meant it when I said I wanted to remain friends with you Jack. I didn't want to break off, not at all."

She took his hand and squeezed it, smiling gaily and a trifle archly; he could smell the damp fragrance of her skin.

"Would you like that – for all of us to be chummy, Larson and I and you?"

"Yes Jack. That would be wonderful. Don't you see? He's very talented and influential. He might be able to help you too."

It seemed to Jack like an off-color joke, but she was serious. "Perhaps there'll be an opening in TV journalism," she continued. "Wouldn't that be a step up?"

"Perhaps."

"Ah, you're not ambitious, Jack, you stick-in-the-mud. Can I make you some coffee? No, you don't take it at night. Anything else?"

"No, thanks Sylvia. I didn't mean to stay long. Just happened to be in the neighborhood.... By the way, the feature is all set. And the Jeff H. plug stays... should be in tomorrow's newspapers."

"That's fine," she said, adding, "But why did you allow that man Nichols to take the byline, after all the work you did? I thought you wanted a byline."

"How did you know about that?"

She laughed a little. "Well, I found out. But I won't criticize you. I'll never do that again. It's wrong to be critical." She walked away from him and adjusted a coverlet on the couch; then she turned to him. "Well, I'm happy you came Jack. And I'm glad you talked to Mark." She kissed him suddenly on the cheek. "Now we're friends again."

He held her at the waist. "Sylvia, I still care for you. I still love you.... But you and I and Mark Larson aren't the three musketeers. That can never be, don't you see?"

She broke away from him. "Love again," she said, a trifle bitter. "The possessive love that sees only itself and feels only itself. Must your love to be so selfish; can't it be big and wide and all-encompassing."

"No," he said dejectedly and turned to leave. But she followed him.

"I loved you Jack," she said. "I still do, really. But it's not a possessive love I have for you; it's not that kind I want."

"Shall Larson and I work out a share-the-wife arrangement?"

191

"Don't be vulgar.... We can go on as before. Have fun. Go places together and do things, but without demands, without questions. Can't you see it?"

She hugged him, resting her head against his chest; her eyes seemed to plead. "Jack, I don't want to lose you again," she whispered, stroking his arm.

"God, I don't want to lose you either," he said, at once unable to control himself. He kissed her lips and felt her respond to his yearning. He kissed her again and again, confident again of their desire, their need, their love. She was right; what were questions and demands when she was in his arms? Then he possessed her and she him and that was all. Their love was as real as any; he had no right to seek more.

With a sweep he lifted her off the floor, holding her cradled in is arms.

"Is it all right?"

"Yes," she replied. "Marsha won't be home tonight."

He carried her into the bedroom like a bridegroom and laid her softly on the white sheet; she stayed motionless like a curled kitten. He knew she waited for him; she wanted him to assert himself; she wanted him to be a man; and he was, yes. He unfastened her bathrobe belt and loosened the thin cotton wrapping. He saw her naked, soft and smooth, vulnerable, waiting only for him....

After the fire of their passion they lay still and in the stillness and the exhaustion Jack felt something had vanished. They were separate again and suddenly the loneliness was excruciating.

"Darling, forgive me, please forgive me," he said, "but I want to hear it. Say that you love me; that it's only me that you love, that you're mine."

"Yes darling, I do love you. Jack, sweetheart, I do love you. You must know that." Then she giggled a little.

"Yes?"

"I just thought," she said. "You know, Larson, he's no good at this." She giggled again, a happy little cry. "He's no good at this at all."

Jack began to laugh too, a slow chuckle that became more intense; she laughed with him. "Isn't it hilarious?" she said.

Jack's laughter increased, his breath came short and his eyes teared. "It's terribly funny," he said, unable to control his laughter, feeling a suffocating pain in his chest. "Oh no," he gasped, his eyes smarting with tears. "You, me and Larson. We are a team... ha, ha, ha, ... We're bound together and can't escape." He wiped his face but still his breath came in gasps.

"Could be," she replied softly; her voice sounding far off.

"There's no doubt," he said, beginning to control himself. "We're all working together. Communism or socialism or something like that. We're frightened of it, trying to keep it away, off our shores. Ha, ha, ha... But it's here, in our midst already. Only people don't know it's here... Or is it only me? Am I the only one who doesn't know?"

"I don't follow you," she said, rising on one elbow. He grasped her hand and felt her quiver.

"Sure you do. You're way ahead of me. We're all doing our little job, see, for the greater good, for the country, for the general welfare. We're forever and hopelessly dependant on each other because, essentially, we're all piece-workers of a sort, doing our little tasks. Who gets the prize doesn't really matter. In the end, we share the prizes."

She frowned and appeared disconcerted but he continued a little breathless, but no longer laughing. "I see it now. The judge depends on the murderers so that he can be a judge. If they're teenagers or adults, it doesn't matter, so long as they do their job, that is, commit crimes. They write the script, but the magistrate gets the headlines. The press agent pens a speech so the Mayor can take his bows. Even pigeons are cooperating and the ASPCA. I report the news so somebody like Larson can deliver it. But then you write a feature so I can get a byline. So I win too, or Nichols does. It doesn't matter. As long as everybody plays the game."

"I don't think life's a game," she interrupted.

"But it is. And everybody's playing. Only some, like me, don't realize it. Everybody does their little job while somebody else takes the credit. But it all equals out because everybody gets what somebody else deserves. It turns out to be what he deserves too."

His eyes glistened; he jumped up against the backboard of the bed. "That explains everything. I couldn't see it before. I suspected you were using me. But Larson pointed out that I was using you too. I thought you had fallen in love with Larson. What a narrow view! Personal and mean. You do love me and not Larson, after all. How funny. How very funny."

"It's not funny," snapped Sylvia.

"Sure it is. Have you lost your sense of humor? Nobody's perfect in this world, but we each have our points, right? Larson's glamor and nightclubs and fast talk and smooth dancing. But on the bedsheets he's a washout. So that's where Stopple comes in. the ghostwriter becomes the ghostlover. It's part of the full employment program."

Sylvia got off the bed and put on her bathrobe. "I think you'd better go," she said coldly.

"What's the matter? Don't you subscribe?" He grabbed her by the arms. "One big happy family. Let's love everybody. Be generous not possessive."

She wrenched free of his grasp. "Get the hell out of here," she screamed. "And don't come back, ever. You're a fool. You're too stubborn and naïve... and stupid! She ran into the bathroom and locked the door. He followed to the door.

"You've forgotten something," he shouted. "I'm the one with the muscles; the real ones. That flimsy door doesn't protect you."

"Get out of this house," she cried through the door. "I swear I'll scream for help."

But Jack was furious. He flung himself against the door and felt the panel shudder. He rushed a second time and it smashed open.

"Keep away. Keep away from me or I'll cut you. I swear it." She cowered in a corner near the toilet, a razor blade in her hand. But Jack stopped suddenly, he had no wish to harm her.

"That's a man's instrument," he said, panting, but beginning to smile at the wild terror in her face. He went back to the bedroom and put on his clothes. He could hear her sobbing as he left the apartment.

A gray and white kitten patrolled the stairs of his brownstone; he recognized it as the landlady's. He stared into its green animal eyes and reached out to stroke its back, but the cat lifted a paw and scratched him. Jack examined the thin line of blood on his hand; then he hissed at the cat and it jumped off the stairway. He started up, tired and sweaty.

As he opened the door to his apartment the telephone rang. "Glad I found you in," said Bill. "I've been walking around the streets and hittin' the bars. I know it's late, but can I come over? I gotta talk to a friend."

He arrived soon afterward. "That goddamn bitch Marsha gave me the air," he said upon entering. "That goddamn fuckin' bitch walked out as if it was nothing' at all. Jesus I'm so mad I could smash something. Gimme a drink, will ya? Anything you got, but bring out the bottle. I need lots of liquor. I'll pay you if I drink too much."

"Don't be silly." Jack located a lone bottle of bourbon in his cabinet and poured a strong shot.

"First she forces me to take her to the most god-awful movie and then, sitting peacefully over coffee and waffles she gets up and walks out. I could kill her. If I only had her soft juicy throat between my hands." He gulped the bourbon and poured himself another.

"What did you fight about?" asked Jack.

"Nothing. That's the damndest part of it. I was just gabbing away and she says 'maybe I'll marry Andre Blaine or not, but with us the movie's over and it's time to clear the trash,' or some shit like that. She admitted she's been puttin' out for this Blaine guy. 'Course that's why I had so much trouble with her. I can see that now. Anyway she just trots out. Imagine how I felt, the whole café watching her exit? What laughter! Brother."

"You can call her again in a few days," suggested Jack.

"Not me Jack. That was it. The End. That lousy whore can come crawling on her nose and I wouldn't care." He took another drink. "I'm terribly upset Jack. I just want to fuck something. Listen, I know a number, a call girl. I told you about her; she's really saved me these past weeks. Let me phone her over here. She'll put out for both of us. And it's my treat."

Jack smiled. "Go ahead. If you need it that bad."

"It'll be good for you too. I know you got your own problems. And I'm payin' and no arguments." Bill fingered his address book and then dialed. "Oh brother, I need some loving tonight…. Hello Monika? This is Bill. I'd like you to come over tonight…. You know me, the Bill on West 23rd, ninth floor,…. yeah, that's right honey, but I want you to come to a different address… What?…. It's $25 now….. Yeah, everything is going up, very funny…. All right, can you come over now? … well, can you make it in a half-hour? … an hour, not tonight huh…. No, not tomorrow night. I'll call you… yeah… so long."

"Too busy," said Bill, slamming the receiver. "Even she's too busy." His voice became shrill. "Somedays I feel the whole world is against me, against us, against all humanity. Even a drink don't help…." He took another swig. "…much. Where's the happy endings?"

"Remember Ann Rawley, the girl who works in my office," said Jack. "She's going to marry Stan Cowels. There's a happy ending for you."

"What," exclaimed Bill. "That character with the gray hair spouting poetry? I thought he was her father."

"Well, you were mistaken. We both were."

Bill pounded his fist into his palm. "So I'm mistaken. Seems all I do lately is make mistakes. On the job…. my crummy love life…" He began to weep. "I don't know what the hell to do anymore… don't look at me Jack… I'm drunk… that's all…"

Bill hid his face in the crook of his arm and wept uncontrollably. Jack came up to him slowly and put his arm around his quaking shoulders.

"…I'll be all right," said Bill, obviously trying to control himself. "I'm so dammed ashamed to be bawling here in front of you…."

"That's okay Bill." Jack tightened his grip on Bill's shoulders; then he playfully ran his fingers through his crew-cut hair.

"I'm okay now," said Bill, breaking away and blowing his nose in a handkerchief.

"Good." declared Jack brightly. "Then Dr. Stopple prescribes pushups, immediately."

"Oh cut it out," said Bill, a trace of a smile on his lips.

"I'm serious. Lie down on the carpet."

"Don't give me the exercise routine now," pleaded Bill.

"It's good for you. Believe me. It's dependable. Come on, I'll join you."

Grumbling, Bill removed his jacket and stretched out on the rug. "Okay, straight back, firm grip, let's go," said Jack. They began pushing up from the floor, their bodies in quick rhythm, their arms straining with each repetition. Three... four... five....

"So what's the answer... knock yourself out with exercise?" demanded Bill.

Up and down, up and down, up and down, the strain increased as they propelled away from the floor and then released the pressure on their arms and came down again. Seven... Eight... Nine....

"Stay in line," said Jack, his breath coming in gasps, "and do what you can.... Or maybe quit.... But be your own man."

"Your own....." Bill repeated.

They stopped talking; their thoughts blurred and the room seemed to fade away. There was only the effort, the constant toil increasing, increasing as they pushed up, up, away from the earth, up, up, only to collapse again, to be yanked down again, up, up, up away from the petty problems, the enormous struggles, the stratagems that circle like colorful ponies on a giant merry-go-round. Eighteen... nineteen... twenty.... Twenty-one.... There was no victory, only the battle against defeat, only the striving, the endless striving.....

"I've had it," gasped Bill. "I'm dead."

"No," responded Jack. "Keep going. Keep going. Life is just beginning."

The End